Tales of the Were
Lick of Fire

Phoenix
Rising

BIANCA D'ARC

DEDICATION

I'd like to dedicate this book to my dear old Dad, who will never read it! LOL! But who went through a bit of an ordeal with a ruptured appendix while this book was being prepared for publication. It hurts to see the ones you love suffer and I'm just thankful he came through the surgery and hospital stay with his usual aplomb. It's physical therapy for him now, and lots of rest as he gets back in shape. With any luck, by the time this book is released, he'll be back up to his old tricks.

I'm very grateful to still have him in my life and I'm thankful to my fans who have been so supportive as I learn how to be Florence Nightingale on a very small scale. Hugs to you all!

CHAPTER ONE

Lance didn't know what was going on with him lately. Fire itched under his skin, and the desert called as never before. He wanted to just go out into it and... What? Self-immolate? Fly like sparks up into the blazing sun? Lay down and die, only to be reborn in the burning heat?

And where the *hell* were these thoughts coming from?

He'd always been a little...odd. He'd had a hard time growing up and in school. He'd been one of the *bad* kids. The kind who grew up to ride a motorcycle and live on the outskirts of town in what was basically an industrial area. It wasn't that he was stupid. Far from it. He'd hidden his intelligence from the other kids and tried to fit in at first, when he was little, but he'd soon tired of it all and just started acting out. He'd become the loner. The recluse. The kid everyone thought was a mental case.

Everyone except maybe Tina. The girl with the sad eyes who watched him almost constantly. Her gaze had made his shoulders itch all through senior year, though they'd never said more than a few words to each other.

She wasn't one of the popular girls, but she had a group of quiet friends with whom she hung out. They didn't mix with him, and he stayed well clear of them, but he noticed her watching hm. A lot. And he couldn't help but be intrigued by the fact that the pretty, shy girl seemed to be attracted to the bad boy biker.

He hadn't acted on it. No, he wouldn't do that to her. The idea of contaminating her with his inner turmoil didn't sit well with him. Maybe he wasn't such a bad guy, after

2

all.

But thinking about high school and the girl he hadn't seen in years was getting him nowhere. Lance got on his bike and set out across the desert, riding the lonely highway to god-only-knew-where. He had an itch under his skin that only the sun and wind might cure.

*

Tina couldn't believe her luck—all of it bad, lately. She'd been enduring one minor calamity after another for a while now. The latest was being broken down on the side of a lonely stretch of highway in the middle of the desert. Great. Just great.

She got out and opened the hood of the car, wondering if there was some sort of magic that might help her get the mechanical beast going again. She was staring at the metallic innards of the engine when it roared.

Okay, it wasn't *her* engine that roared, but she definitely heard an engine roaring. She looked up to find a motorcycle headed her way. She wondered if the driver would stop. Then, she wondered if she wanted him to stop. She was way out here all alone, after all. Taking help from a stranger—one who drove a motorcycle that roared like the devil—might not be the wisest move.

Regardless of her feelings, the bike started slowing, coming to an eventual stop behind her recalcitrant vehicle. Something about the rider's aura seemed familiar, but that was ridiculous. He was still a good ten yards away when she thought she recognized his walk. She remembered that walk...

Holy crap. It *was* him. Lance Fiori. Her high school crush. And, damn, he'd filled out really well over the intervening years. Tall, with golden blond hair and a smile that could set girls' hearts aflutter, he was even more handsome now, if that were possible. Now, if he smiled, she figured she might just melt into a little puddle at his feet.

The chiseled jaw was the same. The determined set of his shoulders as she remembered. The magic she had always sensed in him was a little closer to the surface now. She wondered how that had played out for him. She hoped he'd come to terms with the wild energy inside him and was stronger for it. He'd always seemed a little lost to her in high school, though they'd never really interacted. The large size of their graduating class had made it easy enough to avoid him, and he'd never sought her out—much to her secret disappointment.

But, now, here he was, her knight in shining armor, as it were. He even had the trusty steed, albeit a mechanical one. She wondered if he'd recognize her.

Tina took off her sunglasses and tried not to squint as he drew closer. She got her answer when his step faltered a bit. He *had* recognized her! His next words proved it.

"Tina Bradbury?" He made it sound like a question, but she knew he was just as certain as she was.

He came right up to the side of the car, looking at her as she faced the engine, and met her gaze. He lowered his sunglasses, as well, giving her a peek at those startling blue eyes that had always reminded her of the sky at its brightest. Energy crackled in his irises. Magic and power. Little lightning bolts that only she could see.

"Lance," she acknowledged him, her voice was a little breathless, but she was powerless to do anything about it. "Fancy meeting you here."

"Stranger things have happened," he

agreed easily. "I'm just not sure where or when." He sent her the rare dimpled smile she'd only seen a couple of times before.

She was glad her hands were still gripping the edge of the car because that sinful smile made her knees go weak. Wow. The boy had been the stuff of teenage fantasies, but the man he'd grown into was another beast altogether. His aura was potent. Secure. More intense than it had been at eighteen. Way more intense.

"So, I guess you're stuck. Mind if I take a look?" Lance asked politely.

Tina moved aside as he walked around the car so that he faced the engine head on. He touched a few things and checked a dipstick or two, keeping his own counsel, except for asking her a few pointed questions about what had happened just prior to her breakdown. He scowled a few times, and his overall expression was a frown when he stood back from the engine.

"What's the verdict?" she asked nervously.

"Well, this car isn't going anywhere until it gets a few new parts and some fluids." He launched into a technical explanation that she just about followed.

Apparently, she'd let one of the necessary fluids for the engine get too low—or maybe it boiled off somehow—which caused some small, but essential, parts to break. In short, the engine needed major repairs to get going again, which left her effectively stranded in the middle of the desert.

"Where were you headed?" he asked, looking from her to his parked motorcycle and back, speculatively. "I could maybe give you a lift."

She had to swallow hard before she could answer. The thought of riding on the back of his motorcycle brought that weakness back to her knees.

"I am running late for something. I just need to get back into town and drop off a package, but it's pretty important that it gets there on time," she told him. "I'd be grateful for lift, if you're sure you don't mind."

"How big is the package?"

"Small. It's in my purse," she told him.

"Okay, then," he said, closing the hood decisively. "Let's leave a quick note on the dash in case anyone comes along, so they know this situation is being dealt with, and we can be on our way."

She liked the way he seemed to know

exactly how to handle things. That hadn't changed about him. He'd always been fairly resolute, even as a teenager. She'd liked the way he'd stood up for himself, even back then.

She scrambled in her purse for a piece of notepaper from the back of her date book and scribbled off a note, which she placed under the windshield wiper. She then checked the back of the car for anything she couldn't leave behind. Luckily, she kept her car neat out of habit. All she needed was her purse.

Tina closed the doors and headed toward the motorcycle where Lance was waiting for her. He had an extra helmet in one hand that he must've taken out of one of the big saddlebags. He looked at her dubiously.

"Have you ever been on a bike before?" He looked her up and down, his gaze piercing. Was it wrong that she felt his gaze like it was some kind of invisible caress?

"Um…no. But I'm eager to try," she told him, trying to show some enthusiasm. She wasn't about to turn up her nose at his mode of transportation. He was saving her a lot of trouble, after all.

He chuckled and moved closer to her,

plunking the big helmet down over her head. "This will help. Keep the face shield down unless you like bugs in your teeth," he told her, giving her another one of those rare smiles.

He then took her shoulder bag out of her hands and lengthened the strap to its full capacity before lowering it over her helmeted head and sliding it around so that the bag rested against the small of her back.

"It'll ride easier this way," he told her.

Lance led her over to his bike and got on, then gestured for her to do the same. It wasn't as easy as he'd made it look. Of course, he was a lot taller, with longer legs than she had. Tina managed to hop on, resting her butt on the little pad behind him. She arranged her bag at her back, marveling at the fact that he'd been right about it resting easy back there. She adjusted the strap a bit, but then, she wasn't sure where to put her hands.

Lance solved that mystery by the simple expedient of reaching back and grabbing both her hands. She jumped a little but realized he was just being efficient. He'd put on his own helmet while she'd been fiddling with her bag, so it wasn't as easy to talk to each other. He placed her hands around his middle and patted them once, as if in reassurance. He then seemed to look down and nodded at the placement of her feet on the little doo-dads she'd found that seemed the logical place. She must've guessed right.

Lance half-stood, and she loosened her grip on him as he restarted the beast beneath them. Once he had the engine going, he sat back down and waited for her to put her arms back around him before he put the bike in gear and started off.

He went slowly at first, letting her get used to the movement of the bike under them. He was a considerate guy for all his bad boy looks. She would never have gone off with anyone else like this, but she had always had a soft spot for Lance. Her instincts had pegged him as one of the good guys long ago, and her instincts were never wrong. There was nothing in the mature Lance's aura that made her think anything had changed as far as his basic nature. If anything, he'd become even more of a good soul in the time since they'd last crossed paths, but she sensed a great deal of confusion just under the skin. Maybe…just maybe…she could help him sort that out.

Or maybe, she was daydreaming again. The very fact that she had, at this very moment, her arms around her high school crush seemed to indicate that daydreams could come true—it just wasn't all that probable. He'd take her back to town, and they would part ways. It might be years before she saw him again—if ever.

On that depressing thought, she decided to just enjoy herself in this moment. It wasn't every day a girl got to fondle a bad boy on a motorbike. In fact, such things never happened to plain old Tina Bradbury, the girl voted most likely to have her nose in a book.

CHAPTER TWO

Lance could hardly believe that he had shy Tina Bradbury on the back of his bike. Her arms tightened around him as they took a curve, and she flowed with him as if they'd done this a million times before. She was a natural, shocking as that was to consider.

He'd watched her in high school. Or, perhaps it would be more accurate to say he'd watched her watching him. He'd often caught her pretty green eyes following his every move when she thought no one was looking. He'd had a sort of sixth sense about it. He always knew when he was being watched.

That she was gorgeous and didn't seem to know it had helped boost his self-esteem a bit. The other guys left her alone because she gave off a powerful vibe that was intimidating to fragile young male egos. That long, wavy chestnut hair and stunning green eyes made her a bit too much for a young man to handle. The fools who tried—mostly the blustery guys who thought they were God's gift, and weren't—got cut down by her rejection. The regular guys saw that and headed the other way. Still, she was the beauty of the school, even if she didn't wield her potential power in any deliberate way. The fact that she seemed so unaware of her own looks made her all that much more attractive—and scary.

Like most of the guys, Lance had stayed far away from the tempting Miss Tina. He'd known all along that he wasn't nearly good enough for her. Plus, there was something a little spooky about her. Every time they'd gotten close, he'd felt a sort of buzzing against his awareness—as he was, even now—that he couldn't explain. It was like she had an electric current running through her body, and he was the only one who could detect it.

Lance still had no idea what that was all about. He wasn't one to believe in superstition or myths. He was a practical guy. He'd had to be. He was an orphan who'd grown up in foster care. When someone had been through what he'd been through at such an early age, they either got tough or got crushed.

Lance had decided, long ago, he'd never get flattened by life, by his circumstances, or by anything else. He'd survive whatever life threw at him, no matter what.

Only… That goal wasn't seeming so easy lately. He'd gone out to the desert, not sure why he'd bothered, only that he needed the wind in his face, the sun on his shoulders, the heat in his belly. He'd walked in the badlands by himself for a couple of hours, not sure if he was actually going to get on his bike and go back this time. He'd fought inner demons he didn't really understand, but he'd managed to get back on the motorcycle.

He'd headed on down the road, back toward civilization…and salvation from those inner demons. At least, for a while. And then, he'd spotted her—Tina fucking perfect Bradbury, of all people—broken down on the side of the road. Lance wasn't a big believer in coincidence. Whatever insane gods had put Tina on his path that day might just have given him the kick in the pants that he needed to get his head back on straight.

Or not. He still didn't quite know how it was all going to work out.

One thing was for sure, though. He really liked having her arms around him. For the first time in a long time, he felt grounded. Secure. Part of the Earth, not hovering above, waiting to fly away. Odd as it all seemed.

Lance had no idea where the imagery in his head was coming from. It was so damned strange.

He tried to focus on reality at all times. He had never allowed himself to be a dreamer. Dreamers were suckers, and Lance had resolved, long ago, that he wasn't going to be one of them. Not by a long shot.

But the reality of right now—being on his bike with Tina's arms around him—made him want to dream for the first time in a very long time. He thought about what it would be like if she moved those little fingers of hers over his body in a sensual caress. He wanted to dream about her taking him and allowing him to make love to her. He wanted to fantasize of what it would be like to have her in his bed for always.

Whoa. Always? What the actual fuck?

They drove into the outskirts of town, and Lance realized he hadn't actually found out where she needed to go. *Stupid, buddy. You were so eager to get her on the back of your bike you weren't thinking straight.*

Instead of heading blindly into the center of the city, he detoured to his shop on the outskirts of town. They'd stop there for a few minutes while he found out where she wanted to go, and maybe they'd switch to a car, if she couldn't handle being on the back of the bike with him in traffic.

Yeah, that sounds like a reasonable excuse. Lance congratulated himself on his ingenuity. He was stopping at his shop for *her* comfort, not because he had some weird need for her to see what he'd done with his life since graduating high school.

Tina wasn't sure where they were heading when Lance turned off the main road, but she wasn't too worried. Lance was innately good. She knew that much. He wouldn't be taking her anyplace dangerous, no matter how industrial the area seemed.

There were businesses all around, and he drove right through a large metal gate that stood open, as if for his arrival. The yard was huge and filled with all types of vehicles. Very high-end vehicles. Foreign. Custom. Race cars and luxury cars. It looked like he had one of everything she'd ever seen on those rich-and-famous shows she sometimes caught while channel-surfing late at night when she couldn't sleep.

He expertly guided his motorcycle through the yard and pulled up in front of what must be the office. It was utilitarian, but clean and nicely furnished from what she could see from outside. Lance stopped the bike and gestured for her to get off. After she had both feet on the ground again, he joined her. They took off their helmets in near unison.

"Sorry for stopping here, but I realized I hadn't asked where, exactly, you wanted to go," he said, surprising her. She hadn't even realized that she hadn't given him such an important piece of information. She laughed, shaking her head as he went on. "I also thought you might feel a little more comfortable on four wheels instead of two, but that's totally up to you."

"Is this your place?" She looked around, impressed anew at the setup. It was some kind of exotic car lot, but to what end, she couldn't quite figure out.

"Yeah," he answered, sounding nonchalant. She looked at him and realized he was far from it. His aura darkened as if he was actually concerned about what she might think. "I do custom work for select clients."

"Engine work? Or body work?" she asked, sincerely interested.

"Both, actually," he replied, looking at her more closely, as if surprised that she would ask.

"You have an impressive array of vehicles here. You must have one heck of a client list."

Lance shrugged. "Word gets around, and more people come. I've had to hire a few guys to help keep up."

As if mentioning his employees conjured them up, two guys came around the corner of the building at that moment and waved in a friendly manner before heading to one of the parked vehicles. They got in and moved the car around the back, out of sight. There must be workshops back there. The lot was even bigger than she'd first thought.

"It mostly runs itself these days," he went on, shrugging as if it didn't matter much to him, but she knew it did.

There was a feeling of pride in the spaces between his words. He was right to be proud of what he'd built here. She knew his origins. He hadn't started with much. What he had now, he'd earned. It was truly impressive.

"So, two wheels or four?" he asked, looking at her speculatively.

"Maybe…four?" She gave him a crooked smile to go with her tentative words. "Not that I didn't enjoy my first motorcycle ride, but now that I'm back on two legs, four wheels seems like the safer bet. Or, I could call for a cab if you're busy. I really appreciate you bringing me this far."

"It's no problem. I can take you the rest of the way."

"You don't even know we're I'm going yet," she cautioned him playfully.

"That's okay. I never abandon damsels in distress to their fate. And, I can send one of my guys with the tow truck to bring your car back here, if you want." He gestured toward a shiny tow truck sitting in one corner of the yard that she hadn't quite noticed yet. The truck looked nicer than her car.

"I honestly don't think I could afford a place like this. It's pretty clear you cater to high-end clients." She looked around at the fancy cars parked in the lot again.

"Don't let the flash fool you," he said quietly. "They're not mine. I just work on them. I don't mind an honest, hard-working engine. Your car is basically sound, except for the fact that you neglected her."

"It's a *she*, is it?"

"Most cars are female," he quipped. "Like boats. Trucks are male. Maybe."

She laughed at the nonsensical conversation while he ushered her into the office. There was a desk with a bright-eyed young woman behind it answering phones and doing paperwork. She looked up when they entered, and Tina saw the telltale swirl of magic in the girl's aura.

Shifter. The girl was a shifter. Tina blinked.

It wasn't unheard of to run into shifters in the Phoenix area, but Tina didn't really expect to find one working at such a pedestrian job. And in such close proximity to Lance. Did the girl-shifter know what sort of magic Lance had? Was there something going on between the two? Tina felt a sudden stab of sadness at that idea.

"Hey, Lexi, this is Tina," Lance introduced them. "She's an old friend. Her car is stuck out on the highway. See if you can get Joe and Pete to go take a look and bring it back." He leaned over the desk and wrote down the location, make and model of the car for his employees.

"Sure thing, boss," Lexi said, a hint of curiosity in her gaze as she watched Tina.

No jealousy that Tina could sense. So, Lexi and Lance weren't involved. Satisfaction roared through Tina in an unseemly way. She had no claim on Lance. She shouldn't be so glad he wasn't seeing the pretty young shifter girl.

Lance kept walking into the back of the building, motioning for Tina to follow. He led her into a large office cluttered with stuff that just had to be his. There were plans for engines. Drawings and mechanical parts placed on a large conference table, as if he'd been going over them with someone not too long ago. There was also a drafting table set up for drawing and a large-scale schematic that looked about half-finished. Tina walked over to it.

"This your work?" she asked, truly intrigued. She hadn't known he had an artistic or scientific side. He must've worked hard to hide it while they'd been in school.

"After high school, I went out on my own and got a mechanical engineering degree at Carnegie-Mellon, back East," he admitted in a quiet voice, as if daring her to laugh or disbelieve his claim. She did neither.

"That's amazing, Lance. I always suspected you were one of the smartest kids in our class. You just didn't want anyone else knowing it."

He shrugged. "It was easier to blend in than to stand out."

She thought she understood, though she hadn't faced quite the same challenges he had growing up. She'd had a supportive family. He'd been an orphan. That had always bothered her. A boy like Lance should've had all the love in the world in his life. Instead, he'd always seemed so alone.

"Now, where is it you need to go and how soon do you need to be there?" he asked, his tone businesslike.

She gave him the address, and he nodded, saying he knew the area well enough to get her there. "As for time, I just have to be there before quitting time at five. So, I have about an hour and a half."

"Enough time for a tour?" he asked with only a hint of hope in his tone, though she suspected he was eager to show off his domain to her for some reason. "Or not, if it's not your thing," he said quickly, hedging his bets.

"Oh, no. I'd love a tour. I doubt I'll ever get a chance to be this close to so many pricey cars ever again. I'd like to see what you do with them," she told him honestly. It's not that she didn't like nice cars. It's that she couldn't afford anything better than the jalopy that had broken down on the side of the highway.

And so began one of the most interesting half hours she'd ever spent. Lance was at her side throughout, pointing out different things in the multiple buildings that made up his empire. He had his own giant paint booth and even his own car wash. He had multiple bays where mechanics worked on a much larger number of vehicles than she had imagined. This was a really big operation.

And almost every single one of Lance's employees was a shifter of some sort. At least, every one that she got close enough to really look at was definitely a dual spirit. Shifters. Everywhere.

There was no way Lance didn't know. When they got back to his office at the end of the tour, she felt she needed to say something. He had to realize—after all this time—that they were both part of the magical world, even if he hadn't fully grown into his power back in high school. Neither had she. They'd just been kids, not really knowing their place in the world.

It was pretty clear that Lance had to have figured out where he fit in. Otherwise, how could he have attracted so many shifters to work for him? For all she knew, he was their Alpha!

The thought stopped her in her tracks. She turned on him and just blurted it out.

"Are you their Alpha?"

Lance stopped short, a quizzical expression on his face. "Their what?"

"That's not going to work, Lance. You've gathered too many shifters around you to not be one of them. So, what are you? A wolf? They like having their Packs around them, I hear. Or some kind of big cat? I know the Southwest is teeming with cougar shifters, but I thought they usually stuck pretty close to Las Vegas."

"I have no idea what you're talking about," Lance protested.

"Seriously?" She shook her head. "Look, it's okay. I'm a witch. I've known for a long time that you had magic. I just didn't know what kind, and I was too shy and too unsure of my own powers in high school to approach you."

"I have what, now?" Lance seemed truly confused. Could it be possible...?

"No way." She walked a short distance away. "Do you really still not know?"

"Know what?" He looked confused and a little angry, at this point, but she was beyond being afraid. Lance would never hurt her. She knew that in her bones.

"This..." She lifted her hand, palm upward, and allowed a bright ball of energy to form in her palm. She watched carefully as his eyes widened. "Have you really never seen a manifestation of magic before?"

"Magic?" he repeated, watching the power in her hand as if it were fascinating in some way.

"Magic," she confirmed, walking toward him slowly and taking his hand with her free hand.

There was a little tingle as their energies connected, and she knew it would be okay. His magic wasn't rejecting hers. On the contrary, it was like they were oppositely charged magnets—attracting each other. Wow. Now, that was different.

She transferred the white ball of cool energy she had called to his palm, holding his hand up and coaxing the little ball of energy to go to him. It went and was enveloped in a golden flame as his power answered. It flared up and made them both jump a little, but she held his hand throughout, containing the magic as best she could.

She hadn't expected the flare of his magic to be flame. It was almost the exact opposite of her ice, which she hadn't counted on. No wonder she'd always been so attracted to him. They were opposites, and like those magnets she'd just thought of, they attracted. *And how* they attracted.

"What the hell was that?" Lance sounded uncharacteristically nervous.

"You've never seen your own magic

before, have you?" she asked him, taking pity and dousing the little ball of ice, which made his flame retract, as well.

"My own..." he trailed off, seeming unable to finish the sentence.

"Magic," she said to encouragingly. "I've sensed it in you since we were kids."

"So, *that's* why you were always watching me?" he asked, making her blush with embarrassment and move to put some space between them.

She looked down as she answered. "I'm sorry if I made you uncomfortable. I wasn't all that sure of my own power, back then, but I could always see auras. It's only gotten stronger as I got older and learned control. That's how I saw that everyone out there in your shop is a shifter. Even Lexi at the desk. You really didn't know?"

"What's a shifter?"

Oh, Goddess. He was still totally clueless. Tina felt a little amazed that, at least in this, she was way ahead of Lance.

"*Shapeshifter*," she said, emphasizing the word. "You know. People who can turn into animals and back again."

"You mentioned wolves. Like *were*wolves?" His voice rose on the last word.

He still seemed to be having trouble believing, but it looked like, somewhere inside him, understanding was dawning.

"Got it in one," she told him. "There are all sorts of werecreatures. Birds, cats, bears, wolves. Those are just the ones I've met. Most are pretty nice people. At least the ones I know."

"Just to be sure, you weren't escaping from a mental institution when I found you, were you?"

Tina laughed at his half-serious question. "I promise I wasn't. I was on my way to a client's to deliver a potion she asked me to brew for her."

"Potion?"

She saw he needed more convincing. She reached into her purse and drew out the vial that contained the potion. It was glowing. Swirly blue light emitted from the clear glass bottle. She held it up for his inspection.

"This will help my client find something she lost. But it only works for twenty-four hours. If she doesn't find the item in that time, we'll have to try another solution." She put the bottle away, and the glow went with it. "This kind of potion really isn't my specialty, but I told her I'd try." Tina shrugged. "Hopefully, it'll work."

"What *is* your specialty?" he asked, as if afraid of what she might answer.

"Now, that would be telling," she said with a grin. "I can see auras, and my power is cold while yours appears to be hot. If you're not a shifter, what are you?"

"I have no clue," he told her, taking a seat behind his desk and putting his head in his hands. "I don't feel normal anymore, Tina. And what you've just shown me…" He sighed and ran both hands through his hair before straightening to look at her. "It should've blown my mind, right? But, instead, it just feels like you gave me a piece to a puzzle I've been trying to solve my entire life."

"You really don't know, do you?" she said quietly, sitting in the guest chair across the desk from him.

"I haven't the foggiest."

CHAPTER THREE

"You know…" Tina's tone was more tentative when she spoke again. "I have some contacts that might be able to help you figure out what you are."

Lance looked deep into her eyes, wondering why she'd been put in his path just when he needed her kind of help. Maybe he still believed in fate, just the tiniest bit.

"What kind of contacts?" He'd hear her out. Maybe she *could* help him. It certainly couldn't hurt to listen.

"Most shifters believe in and serve the Goddess. We call Her the Mother of All. Think of Her as Mother Earth, if that helps."

"I have no problem with a female deity. I'm not a religious nut. I believe in live and let live," he told her, just to be clear.

"That's good," she smiled at him. "Tolerance is the sign of an enlightened mind."

"Thanks. So, what does this Goddess have to do with me and my little problem?"

"Well, the contacts I have are in Nevada, and I believe they'd be willing to help you if I asked. They both serve the Goddess. They are a mated pair, and the female is a priestess. They're the most magical people I know, and they would probably be able to tell you why all those shifters have gathered around you. I suspect you really are a shifter of some sort, even though you've never shifted." She paused a moment, thinking hard. "You haven't shifted, right? No gaps in your memory or dreams about becoming an animal?"

"No," Lance shook his head. "But I keep thinking about the wind in my face and the sun on my back. Like I'm flying." He didn't tell her about the horrific side to his thoughts—the part where he's burning.

"That's good," she said, oblivious to his darker thoughts. "You might be a hawk or eagle shifter. Maybe an owl. I'm not up on all the different kinds of flight shifters there are, but I know there's a concentration of them in Las Vegas, gathered around the Redstone Alpha. You're a bit like him, in a way. You employ shifters of all kinds in your business, just like he does. If I had to guess, I'd say you've got part of a werewolf Pack in your garage area, but Lexi is some kind of big cat, I think. And the big guy who was in charge of your painting operation was a bear. I know a few bears, and he has that same aura."

"You know a few—" He cut himself off. "Tina. You know how ridiculous this all sounds, right?"

"I'm aware," she conceded. "But you seem to be taking it in stride. Or, at least, better than someone who didn't believe in magic. Somewhere deep down, my words are resonating. You have the instinct. You probably always did. That's why you caught me watching you when most regular people wouldn't notice a glace from afar. You're just not fully in touch with it. Once you sort that out, I think you'll feel a lot better. A lot less confused, anyway."

"You really think you—or those contacts in Vegas you mentioned—could help me?" The look on his face nearly broke her heart.

She'd never seen strong Lance Fiori seem so uncertain. So...scared, if it came right down to it. He was in a bad way, and her mission in life seemed to be to help folks who needed it. That instinct was what had caused her to be on the highway in her junker of a car in the first place.

Huh. Maybe fate had something to do with this meeting, after all. It wasn't beyond the scope of possibility that the Mother of All should put her in Lance's path when he was clearly in such dire need of direction.

*

"How is she?" the new High Priest asked the healer mage who had been attending their liege lady.

"Weak," the healer replied. "She will take many months to recover, unless a source can be found to feed magic to her more quickly."

"We've already tapped out whatever

sources of magic we could find in the area. She's run through them like bonbons. Frankly, I'm having trouble finding places to stash all the bodies." The High Priest shook his head. He had to find another way to recharge his lady's energies.

They had a war to start.

"Gabriella has the seer's gift to some extent," the healer reminded him unnecessarily. "She was talking about a disturbance in the desert and a vision of fire. A man on fire, flying toward the sun. It might be just a legend, but if there really is such a thing as a phoenix still around in this day and age, he might be the answer we seek. Power of that intensity would go a long way toward reviving the *Mater Priori*."

The mother of their order, Elspeth's wellbeing was at the center of their focus. They hadn't spent so many centuries of effort to bring her back from the forgotten realm to which she'd been banished to let her starve for energy once back in the mortal realm. Her thirst for magic must be met, and High Priest Ornish wasn't about to let her siphon the life out of any more of her loyal followers.

She'd done so at first, when she'd arrived

back in this realm. She'd sucked the life energy out of everyone present at her arrival. Those who had worked so hard to bring her forth had sacrificed everything to her need. Ornish had stepped up to fill the role of High Priest because most of the rest of the leadership of the ancient order of *Venifucus* were dead at the hands of their *Mater Priori*.

A decidedly unexpected turn of events, but it had worked out well for Ornish. He wouldn't make the mistake of starving her of the energy she needed, or she wouldn't hesitate to drain him of his own considerable power and fling the body into the pit where they'd been stashing all the others she'd run through. They'd been procuring humans with even the slightest hint of latent magical energy to feed her need.

They'd managed to trap a few shifters, as well, but Elspeth's thirst for power was great, and the trip from the forgotten realm had been arduous and draining. She'd been back for months already but was still too weak to rise, much less lead the revolution her followers wanted. How could she lead them against the forces of Light when she couldn't even sit up for more than an hour at a time?

A solution must be found. Perhaps there was something to these visions of a phoenix. Or maybe it was just a hallucination. Gabriella had been known to experiment with the drugs she imported and distributed through her network of dealers. Either way, Ornish needed to find out. And he knew just the witch to send on the mission.

*

Gabriella wasn't pleased when she hung up the phone. Her big mouth had gotten her into trouble again. This time with the High Priest. The bastard didn't want to dirty his hands tracking down her vision, but he didn't hesitate to order her to investigate.

Order. Not ask. Who did Ornish think he was? Jumped up little toady. She should've shanked him years ago, before he'd weaseled his way into the power structure and stepped into the vacuum when Elspeth had obliterated the previous regime.

But he was the High Priest now, and Gabriella was obligated to obey. She didn't have to like it, though. Still, she got her ass on her private jet and headed for—where else—Phoenix. She'd seen enough in her vision to know at least that much, though the coincidence of the name of the city the phoenix shifter had chosen to live in made her itch. Had she been wrong about what she'd seen? If so, she was in for a world of trouble from the order if she couldn't deliver a phoenix for the *Mater* to snack on.

Gabby only hoped she didn't end up on the menu, instead.

*

Tina had parted with Lance, promising to call him after she'd spoken with her contacts. He'd been kind enough to take her to drop off her package, and by the time they'd returned to his shop, her car had been retrieved and was running again. She had offered to pay for the tow and the service, but Lance had refused. Tina had made a point to tip the guys who'd picked up her car and done the work on it, at least.

She drove away, shaking her head at the weird turn life had taken today. Her car purred like a kitten, making content sounds she hadn't heard in years from the engine.

The shifter mechanics Lance had attracted were talented individuals if they could get her old clunker running that well in such a short amount of time. She was duly impressed.

Tina got home and placed a call. She had known Kate for a long time and had met her mate a few times. The dude was a scary-assed cat shifter of some kind with a magical talent that wasn't much like other shifters. Kate had hinted at her husband being something a little different from other shifters, but she hadn't said what, and Tina wasn't one to pry. Still, if Lance really was a shifter, maybe Kate and her mate, Slade, would have some insight.

Kate was the priestess for the Redstone Clan of shifters, based out of Las Vegas. Tina wasn't quite sure if asking for Kate's help meant she was soliciting aid from the Redstone Clan itself. She didn't want to cause any trouble for Lance or draw too much attention to him that he probably wasn't ready for, so she was cautious in what she told her friend.

"He's gathered a group of shifters around him, all unawares," she said, holding the phone close to her ear as she moved about her kitchen, making dinner.

"Did anything feel off to you? Any hint of evil anywhere near?" Kate asked, sounding skeptical.

"Not a whiff of evil to be found," Tina assured her friend. "And I know this guy. We went to high school together. He was always a good guy, if a bit rough around the edges."

"High school was a long time ago, Tina. People change."

"Not him. He's still just like I remember him, only older." And even hotter than he'd been in high school, but Kate didn't need to know that part.

"He seriously didn't recognize the shifters around him?" Kate asked.

"Not a clue, but he took the existence of magic well, and there was this one thing…" Tina remembered the way his power had flared up and still wasn't quite sure what it had meant—other than he definitely had magic inside him. "I conjured a little ball of white light to prove to him what I was saying. I put it in his hand, and fire came up from his palm to envelop it. I could see flames."

"Are you sure he's not a mage? Some

kind of fire talent?" Kate said quickly.

"Pretty sure. He reads like a shifter to me, but not any kind I've ever encountered." She kept thinking about her encounter with Lance. "And he seemed really troubled by whatever was going on inside him. Is it possible he's a shifter who doesn't know how to shift or something?"

"I've never seen anything like that myself. I'll ask Slade. He knows more about shifter stuff than I do. But I've never heard of any shifter species having an aptitude for fire. I wonder if he's a hybrid of some kind?"

"I don't think there's any way of knowing from this end. Lance was a foster kid. I don't think he knows anything about his birth parents."

Silence greeted that statement while Kate seemed to think over Tina's words. Finally, she responded. "Wow," she said slowly. "You certainly don't make things easy, do you?"

Tina chuckled. "Sorry, Kate. I didn't do it on purpose."

They hung up after exchanging a few more words and Kate promising to be in touch as soon as she talked things over with her mate. Much as Tina wanted to call Lance right away, she hadn't really learned anything useful yet that she could tell him. Maybe after Kate talked to Slade and called back, Tina would have the excuse she needed to connect with Lance again.

In the meantime, she had work to do. She had to keep thoughts of her encounter with Lance to a minimum. He was simply too distracting.

Of course, he'd always driven her to distraction. He hadn't done it deliberately, but he'd been such an enigmatic presence in high school. He'd drawn her eye every time they were in the same room. She'd found him fascinating and attractive way back then. Now? He was even more compelling.

There was something a little lost about him. A bit more hard-edged and troubled. As if he had a shadow over him, not of his own making. She worried for him. He seemed so in need of her help. She was almost afraid of what might happen if they couldn't figure out what was going on with him. Like maybe, one day, he'd go out into the desert and never return.

She couldn't allow that to happen. Not to Lance. Not to a man who was clearly a magnet for Others, who grouped around him by choice because he drew them. Like he drew her. There was no other reasonable explanation for the way all those shifters had come into his employ. They didn't collect around humans like that.

She wished she'd had more of a chance to talk to some of Lance's employees. She wondered if they even realized what was going on there. What did they make of his power? Were they even aware of it? Did they just assume he was like them, but really private? Or did they know what he was and were there to…what? Protect him? Watch over him? Keep an eye on him?

There were way more questions than answers, right now, and it was all incredibly frustrating. Tina would have to get some answers before she could put the distraction of Lance completely from her mind, but she wasn't going to get any tonight, and she still had a bit of work to do. Tina turned on her computer and started sorting through the email that had come in while she'd been out fooling around with her car and spending time with the delectable, distracting Lance.

CHAPTER FOUR

Tina's phone rang before dawn the next day. She turned, bleary-eyed, and reached for the demon device ringing to shake the house down in the silence before dawn. Something had to be seriously wrong for anyone to call her at such an hour, so she tried to stifle her annoyance and worry.

"Hello?" Tina croaked, her voice rusty from sleep.

"I'm so sorry to bother you so early but Slade didn't get in 'til late, and if he's right about his suspicions, you need to talk to your friend right away. Before dawn, even." Kate launched right into the conversation, but Tina was having a hard time comprehending because she was still half-asleep.

"Before dawn? Why?" Tina repeated fuzzily.

"If he's what Slade suspects, the sun draws him. You made it sound like he was on edge, right? Well, if so, he might be close to his first shift. If he's the kind of shifter Slade thinks he might be, that's the most dangerous moment of his life. In fact, it could be the end of this incarnation altogether."

"What are you saying?" Tina sat up, putting both feet on the floor as she sat on the side of her bed. "What is he?"

"Slade thinks…" Here, Kate hesitated. Tina took notice, because Kate rarely hesitated about anything. "He could be a phoenix."

The word hung there between them for a moment as Tina tried to wrap her head around the concept. She frowned.

"Aren't phoenixes mythical creatures? I mean, I didn't think they actually existed," she finally said, running one hand through her tangled hair.

"According to my mate, they can exist. They are just incredibly rare. Most don't survive their first shift. Or, rather, they burn up and have to be reborn into a new body. A new life. Just like the legend."

"Sweet Mother of All. Are you serious?" Tina got up and started pacing in her bedroom. She was feeling more awake all the time.

"He's not sure, but what you described seems to fit. Slade's people in Tibet have had experience with many kinds of shifters that you and I might call mythical. He doesn't have firsthand knowledge of any phoenixes in the U.S., but it seems kind of fitting that they'd live in Phoenix, don't you think? Especially if one didn't quite realize what he was. I don't find it strange that he would be drawn to that city."

"Yeah, I've seen stranger stuff in my day," Tina admitted. "So, what can I do? How can I help him?"

"Slade strongly suggests that you get to him before sunrise. If he's close to his first shift, it'll get harder and harder for him to resist the lure of the sun. If he's alone when it happens and he heads for the stars, he'll probably burn up in the atmosphere, and that will be the end of your friend, as you knew him."

Kate sounded grave, and Tina just shook her head, appalled at the idea of Lance dying alone in the sky, nobody the wiser, and no trace left of him. That thought was so sad it hurt her heart.

"So, I stay with him? Watch over him?" she asked.

"Yes. That's why the shifters have surrounded him," Kate replied quickly. "They probably don't even realize it, but they were likely drawn to him. Phoenixes are said to have healing powers and special magic that affects other shifters in surprising ways. But he's going to need more than just those gathered around him, if he's going to survive his first shift. He's not mated, right?"

"Not that I'm aware of," Tina answered.

"That's not good. When he flies toward the sun, he'll need something to ground him and call him back. If he were bonded to a mate or had a family, that might work, but according to what you've told me about his background, he's very vulnerable. He has no one to call him back. You need to try to do that for him."

Stars! How what she supposed to accomplish that? It seemed like Kate was asking her for the impossible. Lance was just a high school classmate—not even a friend. They knew enough to nod to each other, but they weren't close. Sure, she'd watched him for the four years of high school, but she hadn't seen him since, and that seemed like a really tenuous connection to her. Would it be enough to bring him back to Earth if he really was this fabled phoenix shifter?

One thing was for certain. It would break her heart if he died and she could've done something to help. It would probably also hurt if he died on her watch, but she couldn't stand around and do nothing. That so totally wasn't her style. She might've been a bit shy in her school days, but Tina had come into her own as an adult, and she wasn't one to stand by and let things happen. No, Tina was usually at the center of the action nowadays.

It looked like she was going to have to do something to try to help Lance. It was the very least she could do. She only hoped Slade was right, and she wasn't going to sound like a complete nutjob when she tried to explain all this to Lance.

"You need to get to him before dawn, Tina," Kate reminded her when Tina didn't reply. "Just in case."

"Yeah. All right." Tina shook herself. "Okay. I'll call if I have more to ask or report. In the meantime, I'm gonna go and get dressed, and give him a call. Damn. It's early to be calling."

"It is," Kate agreed. "But you have to. It could mean his life."

*

Lance couldn't take it anymore. He was awake before dawn. Again. It was like the sun was calling his name, and it was getting louder as the dawn neared. It was driving him crazy.

He was so tempted to go out to the desert again. He didn't understand any of this. He hardly believed the revelations Tina had made yesterday in his office about magic and the nature of the people who worked for him. He hadn't been able to think about anything else for the rest of the day and had fallen into a troubled sleep. And now, this...

This haunting calling of the sun just over the horizon.

He just didn't know what to make of it.

When the phone rang, it made him jump, but he recovered quickly and picked up the call before it could ring again. "Yeah?"

"Uh...Lance? It's me, Tina. Sorry to call so early."

"It's okay. I wasn't asleep." He was surprised to hear her voice, but it calmed him. In fact, she almost drowned out the incessant call of the sun. "What can I do for you?"

"I just heard back from my contacts in Nevada. They have some rather startling suspicions about your situation, and they didn't want me to wait to share them with you. Are you, by any chance, feeling drawn toward the sun?"

"How did you know?" he asked before he was even aware of having spoken.

"Not me. My contacts. They think maybe you're a very rare flight shifter that has an affinity for the sun," she told him. "Look, can I come over? I'd really rather explain all this in person. You're not married or living with someone, are you?"

Lance was surprised by the seemingly

49

disjointed questions but answered readily. "No, I'm single. And, yeah, I don't mind pre-dawn conversations, if you don't. Come on over. I live behind my shop. There's a separate entrance next to the main entrance to the shop yard. Turn up the entrance marked *private*, and that'll take you right up to the house."

"Great. I'll see you in a few minutes. Promise me you won't go outside before I get there."

"I won't," he agreed, wondering why she'd sounded so adamant about.

She hung up, and Lance spent the next few minutes cleaning up a little. He wasn't a slob, but he had left a few things lying around, and the place looked a little sloppy. Five minutes of putting things where they belonged, and the house was presentable enough.

He put the coffee maker on and sat at the kitchen island, waiting for it to perk.

Surprisingly, the doorbell rang before the coffee finished, and he went to answer it. Sure enough, Tina was standing on his doorstep in the dark before dawn.

"You made good time," he observed.

"I don't live far," she told him as he

opened the screen door for her. She entered, sliding under his outstretched arm and moving into the house. Damn, she smelled good.

"The coffee should be about ready by now. Come on into the kitchen," he invited, leading the way after he closed the door.

Tina followed quietly, and he resisted turning to catch her expression. He wondered what she made of his home. He hadn't had too many women here, so he wasn't sure what the female of the species would think of his decorating style. He liked it. It was all clean lines and metallic or stone surfaces. Sleek and easy to keep clean.

He motioned her to sit at the kitchen island as he took down two mugs and filled them with coffee. "Milk? Sugar?" he asked politely. She declined both, and he joined her at the counter with his own mug of black coffee. "So, what have you got to tell me?"

"It's a theory," she told him. "An incredible theory." She sipped her coffee before going on. "My contact says you might be a… And this is hard for me to believe, but they insist it's possible. You might be a…phoenix."

He took that in for a moment,

considering. "Like a bird that flies into the sun, burning up and being reborn from the ashes? That kind of thing?"

"Yeah, strange as it sounds." She sipped more coffee.

"Doesn't sound like it ends well for me," Lance observed, stalling for time. He didn't know what to make of her words, but somewhere deep inside, the idea seemed to resonate. What the hell?

"Yeah, well. It could be bad if you shift, fly up toward the sun and don't come back. The theory goes that you'd die and reincarnate to a new life, new body, et cetera. My contact says most phoenixes don't make it past their first shift unless they have someone or something to ground them and call them back from their headlong flight toward the sun."

"Is that why you asked me if I had a wife or girlfriend?" he asked, putting two and two together. He'd hoped maybe she'd asked for personal reasons, but he didn't want to make a fool of himself, assuming things.

"Yes," she said quietly. "I also didn't want to barge in on you and any companion you might've had here," she admitted, smiling shyly, in the way he remembered from high school. She'd been such a sweet kid, and so totally out of his league. "But my friend insisted that I come before dawn, in case you…"

"In case I went crazy and flew into the sun," he supplied the rest of her sentence, shaking his head. "The thing is, the sun…" He had a hard time admitting it out loud, but Tina deserved to know. "It's calling me. I hear it, even now, singing to me, luring me out. It's very compelling, and it's getting stronger every day. I'm afraid, one day, I'm just going to go out there and never come back."

She reached over and placed her hand on his, surprising him into looking at her. Those pretty green eyes of hers were filled with concern.

"I'm going to try not to let that happen, Lance. I want to help you. I want to be here for you, just in case." She looked so earnest. So pretty. So caring.

He let the moment stretch, and then, he leaned closer, fitting his lips to hers in the first kiss they'd ever shared. Not that he hadn't thought about it a million times before. When he'd caught her watching him in high school—pretty much every time he'd caught her watching him—he'd thought about what it would be like to hold her and kiss her. And make love to her.

Whoa. He was probably thinking way too fast for such a new re-acquaintance. But she kissed like a dream. Like she'd been waiting as long as he had to learn what it would be like—the two of them, together.

The kiss ended, and he backed off. When he opened his eyes, she was still poised close, a dreamy expression on her lovely face. He wanted to kiss her again, but he didn't want to push. She was special. He had to treat her that way.

Maybe it was his imagination, but the call of the sun was quieter now. It was still there, in the back of his mind, but it was much less urgent. Had kissing Tina done that?

He raised his hand and stroked a strand of hair away from the side of her face. "I've wanted to do that for a very long time," he whispered, not sure why he was speaking. Maybe it was easier to reveal truths in the dark before dawn. Whatever it was, he felt like he had to say some things to her now that he had her here, in his house. "I always thought you were the prettiest girl in our graduating class, but that I'd never be good enough for you."

Her eyes widened. "You were a rogue back then. The loveable bad boy all the girls wanted to date."

"None of them could hold a candle to you, Tina. You were, and still are, a class act." His gaze held hers, a magnetic pull between them that he was finding hard to ignore.

"And you're still a rogue, riding motorcycles and fast cars," she whispered, coming in for another kiss. Yeah. Maybe she was feeling it, too.

Lance moved closer, this time, taking her in his arms. He stood from his stool, and she followed him, moving into his embrace as if she'd been made to fit there. The kiss deepened into something even more serious and profound. Dipping low to cup her butt, he lifted her up onto the granite slab that covered the kitchen island. Then, he made a place for himself between her thighs, all while keeping the kiss going.

It was a smoldering fire that was quenched only by her lips. She soothed his raging inferno of desire into something altogether sublime. She was his equal and his opposite, and she seemed to be enjoying this as much as he was.

She scooted closer to him on the countertop, pressing her body into his. He was going to take things to the next level when the early morning silence was broken—for the second time that day—by the loud ring of his phone.

Lance broke the kiss and just stood there for a moment, resting his forehead against hers. "Damn." He was breathing hard, but so was she. They'd been lost to the world, but the phone had brought them both crashing back to reality. "I have to answer that. It could be something important. Nobody calls this early, except when they really need something."

"I understand," she whispered, reaching for the phone, which was on the counter behind her. She handed it to him as he moved away.

CHAPTER FIVE

Tina couldn't believe she'd just been kissing sexy Lance Fiori as if her life depended on it. Damn. He was a good kisser. And she might've learned a whole lot more about his lovemaking had the phone not brought them both to their senses. Saved by the bell. Or not. She wasn't sure if she was upset by the interruption or relieved by it.

Lance was taking notes while still on the phone. It sounded like some sort of automotive crisis that only he could handle. She wasn't thrilled by the idea that he had to leave—not after they'd just been kissing like there was no tomorrow—but she also understood that he had his own business, and he had to keep that going, not only for himself, but for all those he employed.

When he finally ended the call, she was already on her feet, her pocketbook in hand. She was planning to make a hasty exit, trying to keep what little dignity she still had intact, but he stopped her, putting one muscular arm around her waist.

"Where are you going?" he asked, his voice gentler than she'd ever heard it.

She couldn't quite meet his eyes. "You've got work to do. I don't want to get in your way."

He turned her so that they were standing face to face, but she didn't know where to look. Lance was completely outside her limited experience with men. He was something greater than any man she'd ever been with. He was *Lance*. Her high school crush. Possibly a freaking phoenix shifter. It was all just a little bit too much.

But Lance wasn't letting her get away that easily. He lifted her head with one calloused finger under her chin. He didn't force her, but he also would not be denied. She met his gaze, cringing a little inside at what might be going through his mind.

"Will you come back later this afternoon?" His question took her by complete surprise.

"Why?" The word escaped without her conscious control.

"A lot of reasons. First, I seem to like having you around." His lopsided grin warmed her heart. "Second, I really want to talk to you more about this phoenix thing. And third..." He caressed her hair with one gentle hand as he looked deep into her eyes. "The call of the desert is less when you're around. It was driving me crazy before you called and all while I was waiting for you to arrive, but now... Now, it's much more manageable, for the first time in weeks. It's been driving me a little crazy, if I'm honest, and I didn't realize how bad it had gotten until now. You muted it. I mean, it's still there, but it's way less. You did that, Tina. I have no other explanation. If you hadn't already told me you were a witch, I'd start thinking it now."

His smile invited her to do the same. "All

right," she agreed quietly.

"Will you go to dinner with me? I'll make reservations," he offered.

"Reservations? Should I get dressed up?"

He liked the playful light in her eyes. "Yeah, why don't we? Let's do this up right. I haven't been out to a nice place in too long, and I definitely owe you a special dinner for all the help you've been so far."

"I'd like that," she told him. He felt like he'd just won the lottery. "Now, I just have one more question before I go. Do you have a right-hand man? Some employee or partner in your business that you trust more than the others?"

"Yeah, I guess. Why?" he asked, surprised and a bit concerned by her question.

"Because I think we need to have a contact among your shifters. Somebody needs to know what you're up against, just in case I'm not here and you have a crisis. You need allies, right now, Lance. Is there someone you trust enough that you'll let him or her in on your secret?" Her gaze was serious, her words troubling.

"There's Stone. He runs the mechanics. He's a good man," Lance told her, confident in his friend and employee, but would Stone think they were completely nuts? "Are you absolutely positive they're shifters?"

"Oh, yeah, I'm positive," she assured him. "And don't worry. You don't have to do this part on your own. I'm going to come back before closing time. Maybe you could set up a meeting with this Stone guy in your office for like an hour before quitting time? I'll be glad to break the news and see if he's willing to help. I can also probably tell if he's on the level or not, which is something else we need to establish before we know exactly who you can trust."

"On the level?" This was getting complicated.

"Lance, the kind of power you have inside you is very tempting to magic users with evil intent. If you survive your first shift, you're not completely out of the woods. There may be people out there plotting against you. Like I said, you're going to need allies. The people who've gathered around you have done so for a reason. My contacts seem to think they would be a good place to start in the search for those allies."

"All right," he caved, willing to trust Tina in this crazy business, where he probably wouldn't trust anyone else so easily. "I'll set up the meeting."

"Then, I'll be here around four in the afternoon. Does that work?" she asked, smiling up at him so beautifully he had to bend down and buss her on the lips.

*

At four o'clock, Lexi announced Tina's arrival, and Stone showed up, a rag in his hands that he was using to clean the grease out from under his fingernails. His hands were clean, but he was a little fussy about removing all the traces of his labors before he headed home. Some of the guys teased him about it, but most followed his example. Lance privately thought he must have the cleanest garage in the history of garages, but maybe that was because shifters were more sensitive about things like odors and sounds.

Lance had been thinking about it all day. If a person could turn into an animal at will, wouldn't they have more acute senses than regular folk? He thought that was what the legends said, so maybe there was some truth to it all. He wasn't sure. Yet another question for Tina, or maybe for Stone…if he didn't laugh his way out of Lance's office first.

Lance hoped like hell that he wasn't about to make a fool of himself. All he really had was Tina's word for the fact that there were supposedly a bunch of shapeshifters all around him every day. What if she was wrong? What if he was losing his ever-loving mind? What if this was all a big mistake?

But then, he thought about the kisses he'd shared with Tina. Something that felt that right could never be a mistake.

He'd felt so good all day. Better than he'd felt in a long time. The call of the sun had been so much less. It had been a blessed relief not to have that itchy feeling in his mind, driving him to go out to the desert and…what? He still wasn't sure about this phoenix stuff.

What was he going to do? Sprout wings and fly? Yeah, right. Lance still didn't really believe that sort of thing was possible for him. Maybe werewolves were real. He was almost ready to accept that because there had been so many myths and legends throughout the ages about such things. There had to be some element of truth in there somewhere, right?

But people turning into birds? Flaming birds that fly into the sun? Fat chance.

Although... There were plenty of legends about the phoenix out there. He'd done a little web surfing at odd moments throughout the day and had read some of them. It was the stuff of fantasy. Mythology. Ancient lore that really didn't seem to have a bearing on the world today.

He just didn't know. It felt like maybe... Maybe there might be some truth to it, but he couldn't be sure. Not yet, anyway.

Still, he was troubled enough by the rising and setting of the sun, that he was willing to explore the possibilities. He sort of dreaded the meeting to come, though. What if Tina was wrong about Stone and the guys in the shop? Lance didn't want his employees thinking he was crazy.

"You wanted to see me, boss?" Stone took a chair in front of Lance's desk, still working on his fingers with the clean rag.

"Yeah. Just hang on for a minute. I have another friend coming," Lance told him, going to the doorway to meet Tina on the way in.

He kissed her cheek and whispered in her ear. "Are you sure about this?"

When he stepped back, she nodded. "Quite sure," and strode into the office to look at Stone, seated in one of the guest chairs. "Hello, Alpha."

Stone sat up straight in his chair and narrowed his gaze on Tina. He didn't look friendly. In fact, Lance didn't like the way his employee was looking at Tina at all.

"Do I know you?" Stone said, sounding more than a bit unfriendly.

Lance stepped between them. "Tina is an old friend of mine. We went to high school together. Tina, this is Stone. Now, play nice," Lance ordered them, only half joking.

Tina looked at the open door and waved her hand at it. Lance's jaw dropped as the door slammed shut.

"I'm a witch. I serve the Light," Tina said rather boldly. "And I want to help Lance. He's in trouble, and he needs allies."

Stone seemed to weigh her words before he answered. "What sort of trouble?"

"Do you know what he is?" Tina countered the question with another.

"Not really," Stone admitted, looking uncomfortably at Lance then moving his gaze back to Tina.

"He doesn't know for certain either, but

I've been in touch with the priestess of the Redstone Clan and her mate. They think they recognize the signs," Tina spoke more softly. "They think he's a phoenix."

Stone looked at Lance again, as if measuring him. He paused so long that Lance began to feel uncomfortable, but he refused to fidget.

"Well, hell. That would explain a lot of things," Stone finally said.

Holy shit. Had Stone just admitted to believing in the crazy world of shapeshifters and magic? Son of a gun, but Lance believed he had.

"Like why you and your Pack members were drawn here? Why you feel compelled to watch out for him?" Tina asked quietly. "If we're right, he's nearing the crisis point. If he shifts, he'll need something to come back for…or he won't come back at all."

"Sweet Mother of All," Stone breathed.

CHAPTER SIX

Lance was nervous as the sun started its descent. He was out in the desert behind his house. He'd built his shop on the outskirts of town and put his house behind that, so he'd have a vantage on the sandy scrub land that stretched for miles. It had called to him—like the sun was calling to him now—taunting him. Begging him to chase it as it sank below the horizon.

Once Tina had established the mind-blowing fact that he was, indeed, working with a bunch of shapeshifters, things had happened rather quickly. Stone had identified himself as the Alpha of the group of mechanic-slash-werewolves who were on Lance's payroll. Apparently, that meant he was their leader and could make decisions for the group.

Stone had gone on to identify the other kinds of shifters—the bear in the paint shop and Lexi the lynx up front among them. It turned out there was quite a wide range of Others working for Lance in one form or another, and a lot of their suppliers were also shifter businesses. That was something Lance hadn't even considered.

What had truly amazed him was the way his people had come together to stand with him as they attempted to bring on his first shift under controlled circumstances. The idea had been something Tina and Stone had come up with between them, and Lance was happy to humor them if it meant figuring this whole thing out sooner. He was feeling the pull of the sun more strongly than ever—the temporary relief Tina had given him had worn off over the day, and as the sun started its descent, Lance wanted nothing more than to follow it.

Such a weird thought. He still couldn't really wrap his head around it, but the gathering of his employees and Tina out in the wasteland behind his house said that they certainly believed it was possible. Or, maybe they were just humoring him.

He didn't think so, though. They certainly seemed to be taking this seriously. In fact, Stone had started barking orders to his guys, stationing them around the perimeter of the yard like sentries. Lexi had taken up a position next to Tina, as if watching for Tina to make one false move. Lance had to shake his head at that one. Lexi was a kid, not even out of her teens yet. She was good at answering phones, but a badass, she was not.

Or was she? Stone had seemed dead serious when he'd said Lexi was a lynx. Lance didn't know much about them, but he thought they were some kind of oversized cat with tufted ears. He also thought maybe they lived in Canada, so Lexi must be an anomaly if she preferred the desert. If she even was a lynx. Lance hadn't seen anything yet to prove all the claims Stone and Tina had made between them.

"I'm going to cast a circle of protection," Tina said, coming up beside Lance as they all took their positions.

Lance was in the center of a circle of his employees. Stone stood back, watching, and he nodded at Tina's words as if he agreed with her idea. Lexi followed Tina around like she had appointed herself Tina's guard.

"How are you holding up?" Tina asked as Lance took it all in.

He was beginning to feel light headed from the noise in the back of his skull. He squinted, holding the bridge of his nose. "I'm okay. Just not really sure what's happening."

"Okay. Hold tight for one more minute. The circle will prevent evil from sensing you while you are within it, and it will offer some protection for you and your people," she told him.

He wasn't sure what it all meant, but the pounding in his temples was starting to get unbearable.

Tina shot him a worried look and took off for the perimeter of the circle of his mechanics, sifting something through her fingers and onto the ground as she walked the circumference. He thought she might be chanting or singing something, but he couldn't tell for sure. The noise in his head overpowered almost every other sense at the moment. It hurt like a son of a bitch.

Tina came back to him, and Stone was with her. He reached out to touch Lance's shoulder and pulled his hand back as if he'd been burned. Lance felt hotter than normal, but it wasn't uncomfortable.

"Okay, boss. Time to get this party started," Stone said quietly. "I don't know how your kind does it, but the rest of us have to strip so we don't ruin our clothes when we get furry." Stone gave his guys the nod, and all around the circle—unbelievably—everyone was taking off their clothes.

Everyone, except for Tina. Sadly, he realized, she was really the only one he was interested in seeing naked. He smiled a little at his own absurd thoughts as he caught her eye.

"Suddenly, my entire staff are a bunch of nudists?" he quipped. She smiled at him, but he could tell she was nervous.

"It's the shifter way," she said softly. "Try to relax. Don't fight the sun's song, and when it happens, remember, we're waiting here for you to come back. *I'm* here, waiting, Lance. I want you to come back to me." She reached up and touched her palm to his cheek.

She was cool to his warmth. Soothing. Right.

"I'll do my best," he promised. Then, he bent to kiss her softly, just once. She made everything feel better, and for a moment, the noise in his brain lessened.

He drew back and stiffened. A fire was building in the pit of his stomach and wanted out. Tina, bless her, didn't flinch from him. Instead, she stood there, watching him with those beautiful green eyes that now were glowing with power, reflecting the rise he felt within his own soul.

Holy shit. Maybe they were right.

"Don't fight it, boss," Stone said. "Follow us into the shift. Let it flow over you. Just let it all go…"

And as Lance watched, one by one, his staff went from human to animal form. A fierce lynx sat on her haunches slightly behind Tina, standing guard over the sole human form in the circle. The men all around the perimeter were now wolves, standing guard. There were also a few bears, a fox, and a few other animals he didn't have time to identify with his human consciousness before something… other… took over.

Something burst out of him, becoming him, turning his arms to great wings of fire and his legs into taloned claws. The lower part of his face elongated into a beak, and his hair turned to feathers. The sun's call was triumphant. Welcoming. Luring.

Lance couldn't hold it back any longer. He jumped from the ground and leapt into the sky, beating his arms—wings—to attain height. The sky was his home in that moment as he trailed fire out behind him.

The roar of the wind was all he heard as he chased the sun, wanting nothing more than to become part of it. One with the flame that lived in his soul.

And the power! The strength was like nothing he'd ever experienced. He felt invincible. Magnificent. Completely different than he'd ever been before.

The song of the sun was part of him now. It wasn't something he would ever fear again because he understood it now. It was welcoming him. Singing to him. Calling him brother and son, origin and rebirth. It all made sense now, and he wanted to go to the sun…

But then, he heard something else, and his heart tugged him back toward the Earth. No! He was finally free. He wanted the sun. He wanted to be free. But he also wanted what waited for him far below.

Friends. People who cared about him. Responsibilities that he enjoyed. His beloved engines… And a woman…

Tina. Tina was down there, and her magic was calling just as strongly to him. She was cool white ice in the center of a hot desert. She was ice. He was fire. They were opposites, and they belonged together.

Lance made spirals, heading for the place from which he'd started. He wanted to be with his friends. He wanted to be with Tina, most of all. He liked the sun, but he loved his people far below. There would be time later to seek the sun. Much later.

"He's coming back," Stone said at Tina's side.

He and Lexi had shifted back to human form and dressed, keeping her company as she tried to follow Lance's flight. He lit up her magical senses, but she couldn't see him with her eyes. Her vision wasn't as acute as the shifters' abilities.

"Thanks be to the Mother of All," Tina breathed, feeling an enormous amount of relief.

"Could he really have taken off for the sun and never come back?" Lexi asked, at her side.

"That's what my priestess friend told me. He needed us to ground him. To make him aware that he had a reason to come back," Tina said, watching the fiery trail of magic that was the only trace of Lance. He was so immensely powerful—and so new to the unseen world. "He's going to need us more than ever now that he's out. His magic is a tasty target for the forces of darkness."

"We'll look after him," Stone promised. "He's been good to us. Looked after us when we were on our own. He's given us sanctuary and allowed us to form bonds we never would have otherwise. We take care of our own, and he's one of us, whether he ever realized it before today or not."

Tina was really glad to hear the Alpha werewolf say that. Lance would need all the help he could get while he learned the ways of his incredible power.

"We'll run patrols around his house from now on at night. We won't leave him unprotected," Stone promised.

"Good," Tina said, watching Lance approach. "Though, I'm not sure what he'll think about that. You know Lance. He always thinks he's invincible."

Stone chuckled. "So, we won't tell him. At least, not at first. He's going to have a hard time harnessing that beast, I think. We'll keep an eye on him until he gets it sorted out. However long that takes."

Tina turned a quick glance on Stone. "You're a good friend," she told him. "Thank you for standing by him."

"He means a lot to you, huh?" Stone asked.

Tina merely nodded, saved from having to give a full answer by the rather awkward flight pattern of the streak of magical fire that was Lance.

He didn't so much land as crash, but the wolves were there to catch him. After a few false starts, the wolves realized Lance was too hot to handle, but Tina went over. She had no fear of his magical fire. Her power was ice-like, so they complemented each other.

Lance had shifted to human form once on the ground, and he was naked. The simple T-shirt and jeans he'd been wearing had been burned to cinders by his phoenix. Wow.

"Let's get you back to the house," Tina said calmly, though inside, she was quaking. Lance looked really weak. So much so that he was trembling. She shot a questioning glance to Stone, who had followed at a slight distance.

"First timers are often shaky for a while after. It should wear off with a bit of sleep," he told her. "And food. Lots of food. I'll send someone to get takeout. We know what he likes."

Tina helped Lance to the house, and the others gave them a wide berth. Lance was still kind of hot, but he was cooling rapidly now that his initial magic had been released. It had been like nothing she could ever have imagined. He'd been flame itself, streaking toward the stars, like a meteor traveling in reverse.

He began to shiver long before they reached the house. Dark had fallen, and the outside temperature was dropping rapidly. Plus, he'd pretty much burnt out. His internal fire had been banked to a tiny ember. Tina had to get him warm, so she guided him to his bed. He collapsed into a sitting position on the side of the bed and insisted on wiping his feet on the sheepskin he kept on the floor there. She could always beat the dirt and sand out of it later. Better in the wool on the floor than in his bed sheets.

Once he was satisfied with his feet, he allowed her to tuck him into his bed, pulling the covers up to his chin. A moment later, he was out like a light, sleeping off his first amazing shift into a mythological creature.

CHAPTER SEVEN

Tina answered the back door when someone knocked quietly. It was Stone, and he had a giant bag of takeout in one big hand. He brought it in and plopped it on the kitchen counter for her.

"How is he?" he asked in a quiet, somewhat urgent tone.

"Sleeping. He seems all right," she told the big man. "Thank you for the food, and thank you for helping earlier. Lance has always been special, and I'm glad to see he's got such a loyal group of friends around him now."

"You guys went to high school together?" Stone asked, sounding interested.

"Yeah," Tina replied. "We weren't really friends in high school. I don't think we ever even talked much, but we were aware of each other. Or, rather, I was always aware of him. He had that glow of magic around him, even back then."

"Did you know what he was?" Stone asked quietly.

"Oh, no. Not at all. Heck, I didn't even know what I was until I hit my twenties," she admitted with a chuckle.

"And what, exactly, are you?" Stone's tone was challenging.

"A witch," she replied succinctly. She wasn't going to tell this guy before she told Lance. No way, no how.

"What kind of witch?" Stone kept pressing, but Tina wouldn't budge. She would make one small concession, though.

"Nothing bad," she told him. "Nothing that would ever hurt Lance."

Stone eyed her for a moment, as if considering whether to push further, but seemed to take her words at face value. He backed off, heading toward the back door. "I'm right outside if you need help. I'm taking first watch, then my guys will work in shifts throughout the night. Someone will be available if you need anything. Just stick your head out the door and call out. A wolf will come running."

"I can't thank you enough," she said, meaning every word. Stone merely nodded and headed out, leaving the wafting aroma of barbeque behind.

That takeout food he'd brought smelled darn good. If Lance didn't wake soon, she might just break down and start in on it herself. It had been a long day, and she was getting hungry.

"I heard voices." Lance's words came to her from the entrance to the kitchen. He was up and dressed in sweats. He looked sleepy, and a little haggard, but otherwise all right.

"Stone just brought food. Are you hungry?" She went to the counter and put her hand on the takeout bag.

Lance ran a hand through his hair as he yawned. "I could eat whatever's in there and the bag, too," he told her. "Have I thanked you for looking after me yet?"

His voice had dipped low as he moved

closer, and she didn't resist when his arms went around her waist. She allowed him to draw her up against his body, enjoying the warmth of him through the layer of soft fabric against her hands.

"No thanks are necessary," she told him, wondering exactly what form his *thanks* would take.

"Oh, yes, they are. You've gone above and beyond for me, Tina, and I shudder to think what would've happened out there without you. I came back because of you. Nothing else mattered when I was on the sun's path. I wanted to chase it down. To merge with it. That's all I knew. But then, I remembered my guys and my business down here. The cars I love and the work and the friends I've made. But even all that wasn't enough. What tipped the scales and allowed me to break the pull was you. I wanted to come back to you."

Lance's voice had lowered to intimate tones as he rested his forehead against hers. There was a little bubble of intimacy around them that felt special and pure.

"I'm really glad," she whispered, feeling the import of the moment.

Lance leaned in and kissed her, deeply. It

was a kiss of gratitude and care, tenderness and joy. When Lance pulled back, Tina didn't want him to go, but she knew there were other matters to tend to now that he was awake. Food was the first item on the agenda.

She stepped out of his arms and went back to the takeout bag. "Sit down. I'll unpack this and put it on the table. You need to eat. Then, we have to discuss a few things."

"You're bossy," he observed with a grin, even as he sat down as she'd instructed.

She stuck her tongue out at him playfully, unpacking and opening the containers of barbeque Stone had provided. She got plates down from the cupboard and brought it all over to the kitchen table over the course of several short trips. Surely, there would be enough here for Tina to have a few bites of something, just to keep her strength up.

"Don't wait on me," she'd told him on her first trip to drop off the plates and a container of ribs. "What do you want to drink?"

"Water," he told her. "Lots and lots of water."

"Coming right up." She bustled around

the kitchen while he attacked the food she'd put out.

Tina noticed that he'd put a small serving out of every container on her plate before he scooped a much larger portion onto his own. He'd provided a full plate for her, even as he took care of his own hunger. That was the mark of a true gentleman, as far as she was concerned—and a sign that he cared, which touched her heart.

She joined him at the table after procuring two big glasses of water. She noticed that he had a pretty sophisticated purification system on his tap. She'd seen that kind of thing before, in shifter homes. They tasted the impurities more than regular folk and preferred the cleanest water they could get when they were in human form.

She sat, and they ate in silence for a few minutes. The food was delicious, and after the first few bites to sate her hunger, she slowed down and savored it. Lance was more in the mode of shoveling it into his mouth, chewing a little and swallowing to make room for more. He just kept going and going as she watched in surprise. But Stone had known Lance would be really hungry.

Shifters must burn a lot of calories when

they shift, and the mass quantities of food helped replace what he'd lost, she supposed. Flying like that had to take a lot out of a being. At least ground shifters could stop moving and rest a while, but when you were in the air, you had to keep those wings beating or you'd plummet. Maybe flight shifters burned even more calories than their land-based counterparts. It was a theory. She'd run it by Kate and see if she knew whether it was plausible or not.

When Lance finally slowed down, most of the food was gone. He'd systematically gone back to the containers and cleaned them out, one after the other. She'd kept refilling his water glass too, which he drained with regularity. He'd asked her, each time he went for another of the containers, if she wanted any more of a particular dish before he demolished it, which she thought was very thoughtful, but she declined. It was clear he was in more need than she was, and to be honest, the plate he'd fixed for her when he opened everything had been more than enough to satisfy her hunger.

"Were you able to get any more information on my situation from your contacts?" Lance asked at one point when his inhalation of barbequed meat had slowed to a more human pace.

"I wanted to discuss it with you before I talked to them again. Now that we're sure of what you are, the decision about who knows what and how they hear it is up to you," she told him. "I didn't want to overstep. I mean, Kate and Slade know it's possible that I know a phoenix here in Phoenix, but they don't know for sure, and they don't know the particulars. I wanted to make sure you were okay with them knowing more before I said anything else."

Lance paused, lowering his fork, and looked at her. "Thanks." His tone was pleased, and she was glad she'd decided on that course of action.

Of course, her first impulse had been to call Kate, but she'd reined herself in. She was happy now that she had.

"You know, I wasn't kidding before when I said it was your presence that called me back, Tina. I think that's probably the key. If someone like me doesn't have a strong enough bond to something, or someone, on the ground, there's really no reason to return to Earth. Not when the sun's call is so strong you can feel it with every fiber of your being."

"I can only imagine something so powerful," she whispered. "But I'm really glad you came back. We need you here, Lance. The world needs you."

"What about you?" He gave up all pretense of eating as he faced her and looked deep into her eyes.

Tina swallowed hard. Dare she put her heart on the line here? He had only just come back into her life, and she didn't really know all that much about him as an adult. But…she knew enough. She knew how he lived and the powerful friends he'd gathered around him. She knew he was still as pure of heart as he had been as a teenager. She couldn't *not* take that leap of faith and tell him the truth.

"Yeah," she whispered softly. "I need you, too."

He was out of his chair in the blink of an eye. In the next moment, he raised her to her feet and took her into his arms. His lips were on hers before she could even catch her breath, and then, he stole it again with the most intense passion she'd ever experienced.

She sensed movement but wasn't really aware of her surroundings until she felt the world tilt and she found herself on a bed. Lance's bed. The bed she'd tucked him into a little while before. He'd been naked, then, and he was fast becoming naked again as she pushed at his clothing and he assisted by removing it, piece by piece.

He was also removing her clothes, helping her fling them across the room. She didn't want anything between them. No fabric. No air. No nothing. She wanted to be skin to skin with him and learn what it felt like to be joined with him completely.

She needed him like she needed her next breath. She wanted to finally know what it would be like to be with Lance. Her girlhood dreams come true, only so much better. They were adults now. They had lives and experiences. They were coming together out of mutual attraction and respect, not just teenage hormones.

Although…he sure did make her feel horny as a teenager again. He was so hot. *Handsome*-hot, but also just *hot*-hot. His skin temperature was warmer than a normal person, but she figured that was the phoenix part of him influencing the human part. Her own power often made her cooler than normal, so they were perfect opposites. He warmed her, and she cooled him.

She wondered what would happen when his fire met her icy energy in passion. Would they combust, or would they fizzle? Somehow, based on the way he was making her feel so far, fizzling probably wasn't on the menu. Far from it.

Tina held onto his broad shoulders as he came down over her. There was no time or need for too many preliminaries. She'd wanted him for a long time, and their reunion had rekindled the desires she hadn't fully understood as a schoolgirl. Now, however, she was fully prepared to act on the longing that had never faded. The passion that seemed eternal.

Lance came down over her, blanketing her in his warmth. His magic reached out to hers, twining together in a dance mirrored by their bodies as their legs entwined.

"Do you feel it?" he asked, breathing as hard as she was, caught up in the moment.

"Our magics like each other," she told him, rubbing against him and loving the feel of his skin against hers, his hardness heading toward where she wanted it most.

"More than that. Our souls…" he whispered as he found his place between her thighs. She wanted to know what he had been going to say, but she wanted the climax that was so near even more.

He moved, taking her rapidly from passionate expectancy to the most amazing feelings she'd ever experienced. He touched her everywhere—if not physically, then magically. His power enveloped her and felt like little licks of flame all over her body. Delicious. Primitive. And enticing her to follow him into the fire.

That was really something for a mage whose power generated as ice. Nevertheless, she went where he led and had no regrets when they went up together in his flames, reaching a climax unlike any she'd had before in her life. The gold of his fire and the silver of her ice twined around them, bathing them in the extremes of power and pleasure.

Tina cried out his name, and she thought she heard him call hers, too. She couldn't really be sure, though. The roar of his flames was in her ears along with the shriek of her power.

As she came down from the heights he'd flown her to, she realized he'd been saying something about their souls. She reached out with her magical senses, and then, she gasped. They were connected now on the magical plane. Where there had been two separate entities—one of golden fire and one of silver ice—there were now two beings joined by a twining pillar of silver and gold.

They were bonded.

Had he realized this would happen even before they'd made love? If so, how? Lance hadn't even known what he was until today. How could he have known about the magic that would bind them?

She turned her head to look at him. He'd settled on his back at her side. They were both still breathing hard, coming down from the intensity of their joining.

He met her gaze, his internal flame glowing in his eyes. "You're my mate," he said in a soft, sure tone. As if he'd always known and had just been proven right.

"Mate? How do you know about shifter mating?"

She had no idea where he'd heard anything about the bonds shifters were said to form with one special person. And she wasn't even sure if that's what this was. It sure seemed like maybe it was, but she'd need to ask Kate to be sure.

"I had a talk with Stone. He explained a few things," Lance said with a hint of smugness in his voice. He turned on his side and put one arm around her waist, drawing her closer. "Who, other than my mate, could pull me back down to Earth, away from the sun? The drive to just keep going up and up and up, until there was no air and no way back, was so strong. You have no idea," he told her, his expression going deathly serious. "But I knew you were on the ground, waiting for me, watching for me to come back. I couldn't leave you, no matter how strong the draw of the sun. As long as you're here, I will always come back to you, Tina. You're my mate, and that means forever."

CHAPTER EIGHT

Gabriella didn't like this town. It was too fucking hot. Too dry. But she had a job to do, and going back home without something to show for her trouble was not a good idea. A lot of people had been disappearing lately, and rumors were flying about bodies piling up as the task of feeding the *Mater Priori's* hunger for magical power became harder and harder to fill. Gabby didn't want to become one of the missing, though she didn't want to give up the position of power she'd wormed her way into over the years. She'd have to tread carefully.

Either that or give up her goals for the *Venifucus* completely and just stick to the drug, prostitution, and human trafficking empire she was building. There was a lot of money to be made, and in the human world, money could buy almost anything. Then again, if Elspeth had her way, the human world would be changing soon, and Gabby's plan all along was to make sure she had a place in the new order

So, here she was, in the fucking desert, with her skin crying out for moisturizer and her eyes dry as sandpaper. She did *not* do deserts.

But she had her bully boys with her, and they were eager to kick some ass. She liked watching them beat the crap out of people, and she loved it when there was bloodshed to make her a little bit stronger. Blood magic was seductive, and she knew she was just as much of an addict as any junkie her network sold drugs to, only her drug of choice was blood and the magic derived from hurting people. Mmm. Nothing like it.

Gabby licked her lips, just thinking about it. She would bag the shifter and head home.

If she managed to bleed him a bit before they got there, then so be it.

*

Lance felt better than he ever had after the night spent with Tina. The day before had changed him in so many ways. He felt more balanced now. More grounded. Less haunted by the call of the sun that had been hounding him for years now. Everything had come to a head, and he now felt better able to deal with it all.

The guys in the shop had been great. They'd accepted him as one of their own in a way they hadn't been able to do before. They all deferred to him even more than usual, but they also seemed to see him as a kindred spirit now, where before he'd just been the boss.

Tina had left in the morning when Lance went to work. She had things to do, she'd said, but she'd come have lunch with him at the shop. He was looking forward to it. He'd arranged a catered buffet for everybody, to thank them for their help yesterday.

In fact, the catering had just arrived, and

Lexi had taken charge of setting everything up in the big room they kept for client conferences. It had been designed so that they could pull the client's car right into the room from the lot, but it was empty at the moment, and folding tables had been set up to hold the buffet.

Knowing what he knew now about shifters, he'd opted for meat, meat and more meat, and plenty of it. He'd ordered in from a local steak place that was known for their quality. It was a splurge the crew richly deserved, and as lunchtime drew near, he could tell everyone was eager to chow down.

Lance saw Tina's car pull into the yard, and he felt the smile stretching his face. He'd missed her in the few hours she'd been gone. He had so much to be thankful for in his life. Running into her again had to rank right up there with the many blessings he'd received in the past couple of days. Not only did he have a great crew who were slowly teaching him the ropes of this shifter thing, but he had a mate...if only she would agree to it.

He could be patient, though. He'd convince her one way or another.

Lance opened the front door, greeting her

with a kiss as she made her way into the office area. He heard a few wolf whistles but was mostly oblivious to it while he enjoyed the kiss of his mate. Nothing and no one could compare to Tina. Only one night together, and he was already an addict.

Tina heard the wolf whistles coming from the werewolves and knew she was blushing, but she was powerless to resist Lance's kiss. So much had happened in such a short time, she still couldn't quite believe it all. Not only had he made his first flight as a phoenix, but he seemed convinced that she was his mate.

She'd spoken to Kate earlier this morning, and she was halfway to believing it was true, but Tina was going to bide her time. She wanted to make it special when she agreed to be his mate. The doorway of his office space wasn't exactly romantic. She'd save her acknowledgment for a more appropriate moment.

Lance ended the kiss but kept his arm around her shoulders as he escorted her to the big room where the wolves and other assorted shifter employees had gathered. They were all looking at Lance expectantly, as if they needed his permission to start in on the buffet. He paused just inside the door and let her go, turning to face his people.

"I can't thank you all enough for what you did for me yesterday," Lance began. "This celebratory lunch is just one small way for me to say thanks. You guys were always a great team, but now, I'm learning why and how. I assume I'm going to make a few mistakes as I learn about being...what I am..." He seemed to hesitate to name his animal side. "I hope you'll all be patient with me and let me know when I screw up." Laughter and cheers greeted his humble words, but still, nobody moved until finally Lance said, "Dig in!"

At that point, it was like someone had set off a starter's pistol as everyone made a grab for their favorites off the buffet. Stone was overseeing his wolves, but Lexi and the other shifters were in there, doing their best to get the prime bits they wanted before the wolves ate it all.

Lance had ordered way more than he thought they'd need, so he wasn't too concerned about anyone going away hungry. He was content to stand back and watch his people, making sure they were all taken care of before he waded in to get his own plate.

But Lexi, apparently, had other ideas. She hadn't been collecting her own food, as he'd thought. No, she came up to him and Tina, holding two heaping plates, which she offered to them.

"You two are the Alpha pair here," Lexi said with a shy smile. "Consider this my way of currying favor in hopes of a raise."

Tina took the plate Lexi gave her, and Lance followed suit, unsure what to say. He finally coughed up a rough *thank you*, which made Lexi grin wider as she turned back to the buffet to hopefully get something for herself, this time.

"I think you're going to have to get used to a few changes around here, now that you've taken your place among your fellow shifters," Tina observed.

"I'm not really sure what to make of it all," Lance said honestly, heading for a pair of chairs.

There were places to sit all around the large room. He'd had tables and chairs brought in for everyone, and they were all beginning to find spots where they could sit in small groups and enjoy the free meal.

*

"They're all inside, boss," Gabby's favorite stud said, cracking his knuckles. "Some kind of party in what looks like a conference room."

"They didn't see you?" Gabby asked sharply. It wouldn't do to alert the phoenix that she was coming for him.

"Nah. They're all chowing down like nothing could possibly hurt them. They didn't even leave a lookout," he assured her. "And I was careful to stay downwind. Even if there's more than the one shifter, they won't have spotted me."

Gabby wasn't sure she liked her henchman's overconfidence, but there'd be time to cut him down to size later. First, she had to get the phoenix and get her ass out of this hellhole and back to civilization. It was so hard to get good help. Gabby had a habit of running through them, but she couldn't help it if men were so unreliable.

They were good for a few things, though. Kicking ass was right there at the top of the list. She loved watching her boys make other men bleed. She got off on it and recharged her energies with it. There was nothing like a little blood to give her a boost.

It was time she made this miserable trip worthwhile. It was time to hurt or even kill someone or—if she was lucky—more than one. She'd drink in the power from the fight, which would help her subdue the phoenix. If the boys could catch him by surprise and beat the ever-loving shit out of him first, maybe her job of holding his power in check until they got back home wouldn't be so difficult, after all. If he was unconscious, he couldn't fight back.

"All right, then," she told her right-hand man. "Do what you do best. Take them out as quickly and quietly as possible. I don't mind if you kill the bystanders, just leave the boss man to me. He's the one I came for."

*

When the big door from the yard burst open into the room, everyone was shocked into stillness for one frozen moment. Then, all hell broke loose as a team of big men came in, fists swinging, some armed with big knives, brass knuckles, or even chains.

What the actual fuck?

Lance sprang to his feet, as did all his people. He was at the back of the room, but Stone was up near the door with his Packmates. They sprang into action, fighting back with a speed and fury Lance had never seen. Within moments, the fight had rolled out of the room and into the yard where they'd have more room to brawl.

"Lance! Look out!" Tina shoved him to the side, just as a blood-red firebolt would have struck him.

He didn't know what the hell was going on, but now, he was getting pissed off. The newly awakened firebird inside him pushed for freedom. He wasn't sure what he could do as a bird against a veritable army of brawlers, but he was having a hard time fighting the new instincts riding him.

He looked over at Tina—the bolt of what could only be magical energy had split them up. She'd pushed him right, and she'd gone left. He'd have to thank her for that later…if they made it out of this—whatever *this* was—alive.

"Do it!" she shouted at him above the noise of battle.

All the while, she was scanning their

opponents, probably looking for where the mage energy had come from. He saw her gaze zero in on a target a moment before a highly-concentrated ball of icy energy formed between her palms.

She was going on the offensive. That stirred his ire again. Why should his people, and his mate, have to fight for their lives? There had to be something he could do to stop this.

Between one thought and another, the new presence inside him made itself known. The bird burst from him in a flash of orange, destroying his clothing, but he didn't care. All the phoenix wanted to do was protect those who were important to him. Lance let go of his conscious thoughts and let his instincts take over.

Tina was shocked by the attack, but she should have expected it. Lance's magic was a big, fat, juicy target for evil magic users who would try to capture him and steal his power. Tina had been a fool to let her guard down, but maybe they could fight their way out of this.

She spotted at least one mage—a scary looking woman with dead black eyes and curly dark hair. She was positioned behind the fighters, taking careful aim with her destructive energies. The moment Tina identified the other mage, she called her powers to her. That black-haired witch was about to be taught a lesson. But first, Tina would shield the shifters. No sense letting them get in the middle of a magic battle that would be fought between Tina and the other woman.

Tina let loose her concentrated ball of protection, encasing the shifters and their opponents in her own special magic. A glowing dome formed over the fighters, and little by little, they froze in place. That was one of Tina's special gifts. Her magic could totally stop people and things around her— at least for a short period of time. And the dome of protective ice energy wouldn't allow the other mage to harm anyone under it while it lasted.

Good. Tina nodded to herself. Now that the shifters were protected a bit, it was time to take out the trash. Tina called more of her magic to her, forming her next volley. This one would go straight at the woman aiming for Lance. No way that bitch was going to hurt him. Not on Tina's watch.

Tina walked farther out into the yard, through the bubble of her own magic and the fighters who were all frozen in place. They were aware of what was happening and could move their eyes...slowly...to follow the action, but they couldn't really move. Not while her magic lasted. She saw dismay on the faces of the men who'd attacked them as she made a beeline through the frozen fight scene, headed for the witch on the other side.

"If you thought it would be easy to take us down, think again," Tina said, holding her own special brand of icy energy aloft in both hands as she stepped out of the dome on the other side, a few yards from the other mage.

"You think you're going to stop me, little girl?" the other woman taunted.

Tina jerk her chin toward the bubble of frozen energy behind her. "I think I already have. I just missed one."

Ooh. That one had pissed the other woman off. Tina braced for the attack she was sure would be coming after her taunt, but she was prepared. The energy in her palms was ready. She could protect herself with one hand and lob the other ball of ice at her prey. It was a trick she'd used before.

And, just like clockwork, the blood energy shot forth from the other woman's hands. Tina blocked as best she could, but the other woman was strong. She must've been on the blood path for a very long time. Her aura was completely corrupt, and the feel of her magic was oily. Unclean. Tina tried hard not to retch.

After the bolt of blood energy was over, Tina launched her own power at the other woman, but it didn't even make a dent. Tina knew, then, this was going to be a long battle. She only hoped she was mage enough to win.

Lance flew above, looking down on his yard as the woman he wanted like no other faced the interloper. The phoenix shrieked its outrage as he saw the dirty magic through the phoenix's eyes. It looked different now than it had when Lance had been in human form. He could see magic in a whole new way now. He could easily tell good from bad. Light from dark. And the woman with the black hair reeked of evil.

The phoenix flapped its wings, watching as the volley after volley of energy went between the invader and Tina. Tina had protected Lance's flock, but she was fighting a very even battle with the dark woman. Lance had to do something, but he wasn't sure what.

Being a phoenix had to be good for something other than flying around, chasing after the sun. He had to have some kind of power of his own, right? Some way to defend his home and his people...and his mate.

CHAPTER NINE

The black-haired woman was tough—Tina would give her that. She didn't play fair, and her power had the unmistakable taint of blood magic. It was wearing down Tina's reserves, but she thought, on balance, they were pretty evenly matched. The outcome of this showdown was too close to call. Something had to give some way or Tina was very much concerned that she wouldn't be the one to prevail in this battle.

She kept lobbing her offensive energies at

her opponent, each blast weakening her. But the other woman was becoming weaker, too. Freezing the battle between the shifters and this woman's henchmen had been a bit of good luck. Without the violence and bloodshed to feed from, the other mage had only what she'd brought with her to the fight. If Tina's ice shield failed, then all was lost. She had to do something to end this quickly, before her dome of frozen protection started to thaw.

Tina went down on one knee as another blast from the woman took her by surprise and knocked her off balance. She fired her own blast back at the woman from her semi-kneeling position and was glad to see the other mage knocked back a few paces. They were both scoring hits now, in this fast-paced energy battle.

As she dealt with yet another barrage from the blood path mage, Tina thought she heard the phoenix shriek. She wanted to tell Lance to fly far away from this disaster of a battle, but she couldn't spare the energy. She was doing all she could just to withstand the concentrated blast of evil power directed at her.

Then, it lifted. All of a sudden, the attack

ceased, and it was the other woman who was screaming, her fists raised to the sky defiantly, even as pure flame enveloped her from the phoenix. Magical flame that didn't burn anything it touched except for the evil taint that was all around the other mage.

The phoenix flapped its wings, and fire shot forth, bathing the entire yard in an eerie orange glow. Everywhere the phoenix's power touched evil, it burned, leaving the rest of the yard—and all of Lance's people—untouched. The phoenix fire didn't interfere with Tina's ice shield either. It seemed to lick at it, and went right through it in spots, but left it basically intact, seeking out only the spots where the blood path energies had touched, to cleanse the taint away.

The black-eyed woman screamed as she went up in flames. She tried to fight back, but the phoenix fire was too potent. Too overwhelming. Too awesome in its might.

Within minutes, the evil mage was no more, and every trace of her contamination had been burned away. Tina sobbed in relief as she sank to the ground for a moment of respite. It was over. The woman had been reduced to nothing. Even now, her ashes were being swept away into nothing by the magical wind created the phoenix's mighty wings. He landed in front of Tina. A man-sized bird of feathers and flame. A paradox that should probably not exist in this modern world of men and machines.

In bird form, Lance came over to her, leaning down and touching her with his flaming feathers in a gesture of concern. His touch didn't burn. Wonder of wonders... It healed.

Renewed by his presence and relieved that they were safe, Tina got to her feet and stepped into the bird-man's embrace. Lance had shifted about halfway, and the outline of the giant bird of fire stayed around him like a living aura, even as his beloved face reappeared. Tina hugged him, feeling the feathers fade away under her hands as Lance came back to her all the way, to his fully human form.

"Are you okay?" His deep voice sounded near her ear, concern in his tone.

She leaned back to look up into his eyes. Eyes that were still swirling with fiery magical energy.

"You were magnificent," she told him, so proud of him she couldn't contain it. "You saved us all."

"No, sweetheart, you did that. You put the dome over the fighting. You shielded my people, though it must've cost you a lot of power to do it. Thank you." He leaned in and kissed her, a too-quick joining of lips and hearts that they didn't really have time for but needed nonetheless.

Knowing she should release the shifters, she turned to look at her dome and was shocked to see that all the opponents had been vaporized along with their leader. There would be no one evil left to tell the tale of what had happened here today.

"How did you do *that*?" She gestured toward the dome, which still stood, and the frozen shifters trapped within its protection.

"I'm not really sure. It looked like the flames just went for anything that looked bad to my sight while I was up there." He pointed upward with one finger, clearly not altogether comfortable talking about his new abilities yet.

"Bad?" she echoed. "You mean you can see evil?"

Lance shrugged. "I'm not entirely sure. I see things a lot differently when I'm in that other shape," he admitted. "It's going to take a while to figure it all out. I just followed the instincts that kicked in when I got a good look at what was happening below."

She patted his chest. "Thank the Mother of All for your instincts."

Gathering her power back to her, she released the shifters from their frozen state, dismissing the dome of protection. She figured she'd have to face the music now for freezing them like that. Shifters of their strength and caliber probably didn't like having their fight stolen from them. She held up her hands, palms outward in a gesture of peace.

"I'm really sorry, guys," she told them quickly as they all turned to regard her and Lance. "That woman was a blood path mage. The fighting was only making her stronger. It's probably why she'd brought those guys with her armed only with simple weapons. They could have just as easily been carrying guns and taken us all out quickly, but she wanted you to suffer and bleed so she could feed off it. Freezing you was the only way I could stop her overpowering us all."

Stone stepped forward and regarded her a moment. Tina held her breath, wondering if the Alpha werewolf was about to condemn her for what she'd done. Instead, he held out one hand to her. She put her hand in his, not quite sure what was going on.

"Thank you for sparing my people unnecessary injury. We like a good brawl as much as the next guy, but feeding our power to a blood path mage is not something we would do by choice. You made the right call," Stone told her.

She was shocked as he leaned over and kissed the back of her hand, like some kind of courtly gallant. Lance came up beside her and put his arm around her shoulders, staking a claim. Stone looked up, let go of her hand and then backed off, grinning from ear to ear. He nodded to Lance.

"Nice one, boss," Stone said, the rest of the shifters coming up behind him to gather around. "That phoenix fire tickles."

Tina gasped, but Stone's irreverent comment cracked everyone up, including Lance. It was just the icebreaker they needed to relieve the tension.

"You're lucky you're one of the good guys, Stone, or I think it would have done more than just tickle," Tina observed as the laughter died down a bit.

"Yeah, there is that. So, I guess we should figure out how these bastards got here and start erasing any evidence of their visit," Stone said, looking around innocently, as if feeding the next move to his boss wasn't something he did every day.

"Okay," Lance replied. "I... Uh... I guess you can tell I'm not very experienced with this stealth stuff. Can you do that without causing issues down the road?"

"We're really good at hiding our tracks," Stone assured him. "We've had to watch our tails our entire lives. We're expert at it."

"All right, then. Do what you think is best," Lance told his right-hand man.

Stone gave a few signals to some of his guys, and they all took off in different directions. A few shifted into wolf form, putting their noses to the ground like bloodhounds and then streaking off into the desert around the yard.

"Hey," Lexi called from the car-sized doorway that had been smashed in by the evil mage's power. "Most of the buffet is still intact if anyone's still hungry."

Tina heard the laughter and realized this group was going to be okay. They weren't mad at her for intervening. Far from it. And they seemed to know what to do to keep Lance—and all of them—safe from repercussions. Now, the only thing that had to be addressed was ongoing security, but that could wait a few minutes while Stone and his guys did their thing. Tina figured they'd be at the heart of any security planning, since they each had a lifetime of experience in keeping themselves and their people safe.

Lance had gone over to the smashed door and had already begun tearing out the parts that would need to be replaced. A few of the guys who had stayed behind came up to help, and within moments, they had cleaned up the debris inside the room and taken the broken furniture and chairs out to the dumpster. Ace, the leader of the bear shifters from the paint shop, was working with Lance on the door, and two more guys were already sourcing lumber and plywood to close up the hole while they waited for a replacement door.

Tina watched it all, marveling at the way Lance and his people worked together. Lexi had brought two chairs out and then followed those up with some drinks and a couple of sandwiches that hadn't been harmed by the fight. She and Tina sat side by side in the shade of a small awning at the side of the building, watching the guys work.

"They really are a good team," Tina observed to Lexi.

They'd sat mostly in silence, eating steadily. Tina wasn't sure if Lexi realized that, after such an expenditure of magical energy, eating a big meal was one good way to replenish energy. Tina thought it was the same for shifters, which was part of the reason they ate so much and never seemed to get fat.

"Most of them have worked for Lance for a while," Lexi replied. "I came on board last year, but Stone and the bears were here from the beginning. As Lance's business grew, Stone brought more of his wolves into the fold. When I moved to the area and was job hunting, I was sort of drawn to Lance's ad for a receptionist. It was an instinctual thing." Lexi tilted her head as if remembering. "I'm really glad I listened to those instincts because this is probably the best job I've ever had, and once Stone and Ace accepted me, I felt like part of the family, even though I'm the only cat here."

Tina looked at the other woman. "I'm glad you found your place," she said quietly, wishing there were some way Tina could fit in among these close-knit shifters.

"I think you've found yours, too, haven't you?" Lexi asked with a sly smile, looking pointedly over at Lance and then back.

Tina decided to lay it on the line a bit with Lexi. Sort of test the waters and see what at least one of the friendlier shifters might think.

"I hope so," Tina replied, keeping her voice down. "I'm not sure, though. Do you think my presence would disrupt the family vibe you've got going on here?"

"Girl," Lexi scoffed. "You don't recognize how well you've already been accepted? Stone kissing your hand before? That was a signal. You're okay in his book, and he was stating it publicly for all of us to see. I doubt Ace will give you any trouble. Despite how scary he looks, he's really just a big ol' teddy bear. The rest of the bears follow his lead. And Lance…" Lexi looked at her boss then back at Tina, her eyebrow raised. "If you can't see the way he looks at you, then you're blind. Or maybe just in denial."

"Or scared," Tina added in a whisper.

Lexi reached out and put her hand on Tina's forearm in a caring way. "Don't be scared, Tina. He needs a strong woman by his side, and from what I just saw, you're the right match for him. He's fire," Lexi nodded toward Lance, "and you're ice. If you're not meant for each other, I don't know who is."

Lance worked alongside his guys to clean the place up. It felt good to use his hands for something constructive. He was having a little trouble with the idea that he'd just killed a bunch of people. Okay, they were evil people, but still.

The newly awakened bird side of his mind didn't have any problems at all with the concept, but Lance had been raised human. He'd always *been* human. Until recently. It was all just a lot to take in.

His guys seemed to understand. They worked with him to fix the shop, not speaking much. Just working steadily. Doing what needed to be done. At some point, Lance became aware that Lexi had taken Tina under her wing, so to speak, and was taking care of her. Lance should be doing that, but he didn't know how he could touch Tina now that he had so much blood on his hands. It was going to take a little time to come to terms with what he'd done…and what he'd become.

"I think that about does it for now," Ace said, standing back from the boarded-up doorway, surveying it with his hands on his hips. "You want to upgrade to a newer style of door when we replace it?"

"Yeah, I guess so. Pretend like we decided to spruce up the place instead of admitting that we got attacked by an evil witch and her followers." Lance heard the strangeness in his own voice, knowing he wasn't handling the aftermath of his actions well. "And how I blew them all away into dust."

A large hand came down on his shoulder. Ace was at his side, looking at him with solemn eyes.

"You weren't raised knowing what you are," Ace began, his voice low, just between them. "That's got to be a disadvantage to you, right now, but let me clue you in on one thing. Killing is something your animal side does instinctually to survive. At least, that's what my bear does. I'm not sure that a mythological beast like a phoenix needs to kill to eat. Maybe your beast serves a higher purpose. Maybe your function is to stop evil when you see it." Ace gave Lance's shoulder a hard squeeze then let go.

Ace was normally a quiet man. In fact, Lance had never heard this many words in a row from the big guy. But what he was saying made a lot of sense.

"I definitely saw things differently while I was up there. Can you see the difference between good and evil when you're in your other form?" Lance asked tentatively.

"I see in what I call bear-vision. I see in color, but not quite the same as I do in my human form. Things are sharper close up. Things in the distance aren't as clear, but I see them with sort of an energy halo around them. Like a heat signature or something around all living things. Maybe I'm seeing their aura—if such things exist, but I wouldn't say I can tell if they're good or evil. That's something I can sometimes scent, but not see. As an example, those who attacked us today, and especially the woman who led them, reeked of blood magic. As a bear, I'm a little more magical than the others. If you ask one of the wolves, they'll probably say they smelled the blood, but perhaps not the magic. And they see more like dogs—but don't tell them I said that." Ace gave Lance a grin. "You're saying you can actually see evil?"

"Oh, yeah." Lance remembered the way it had all looked from above. He hadn't realized what he was seeing at first, but when his phoenix instincts took over, he'd known without doubt what needed to be done. He told Ace as much.

"That's pretty cool," Ace allowed. "Just follow those instincts, and you should be all right."

"Even when they turn me into a mass murderer?" Lance asked bitterly, unable to hold back his feelings of guilt and shame.

"Son, what you did today wasn't murder. It was justice," Ace said fiercely, a hint of a growl in his voice.

"Who gave me the authority to pass out that kind of justice?" Lance wondered, feeling lost.

"Who gave you the gift of the phoenix inside you?" Ace shot back but didn't wait for Lance to answer. "The Mother of All knows what She's doing, my friend. You are what you are for a reason, and today, you were the tool the Goddess used to bring Her Light to the wicked. You are Her instrument. Trust that. Trust in Her."

Those words set Lance back on his heels.

He hadn't considered the religious aspect of all this. He'd always thought he was human, with human ideas of right and wrong. The deity Ace was talking about seemed to take a much more active and ongoing role in people's lives than any deity Lance had ever heard about in the human world.

Lance might have asked for more enlightenment, but the phone rang in the office, and Lexi rushed past him to head inside. A moment later, Tina was at his side, looking at him with a fond expression that touched his heart.

"You doing okay?" she asked.

Lance was peripherally aware of Ace moving away as Tina stepped closer, but all Lance cared about in that moment was the touch of his mate. Of Tina stepping into his open arms.

"I should be asking you that question," he replied, hugging her close and tucking her head into his shoulder. She fit against him so perfectly there was no doubt left in his mind that they were meant to be together. Always.

"I'm fine," she assured him, her hands running over his back in a comforting way.

"Tina, will you...?" he trailed off, unsure how to phrase what was in his heart. The

phoenix inside him knew what it wanted, and it wanted Tina.

She drew back to look into his eyes. "Will I what?"

He plucked up his courage. "Will you marry me?" he rushed the words together, but at least he got them out. Then, he tried to do better. "I want you with me always. I want your life to merge with mine. The new part of me that was always there but silent before knows it needs you. You are my balance. My strength. My reason for coming back to Earth every time I turn into that fiery bird. I don't know how to describe it, exactly. It's more than love. More than devotion. It's like you're the other half of my soul. I know the other shifters are content to just call each other mates, but until now, I always thought I was just a regular human guy, and I want you to be my wife."

Tina's eyes filled with tears. Happy ones, he hoped, though he was holding his breath, waiting for her response.

"Yes," she breathed through the tears. When she smiled, it about melted his heart. "I feel the same." She jumped up, and he caught her, hugging her close. "I love you, Lance," she whispered near his ear. "And

now that I have you, I'm never letting you go."

He kissed her, then, and it was some time before the cheering in the background registered. When he drew back, he realized the guys in the yard were clapping and hooting and hollering, all wearing big, goofy grins on their faces.

Lance wasn't sure how it had happened, but he seemed to have gathered a large, noisy, fun and fierce family around him. Now, he had a mate and his wild side was out in the open and working with him, the future looked bright, indeed... And filled with love.

EPILOGUE

Across town, a young woman felt the stirring of flame beneath her skin. Something was calling to her. Something out in the desert. Something she didn't understand and was afraid to acknowledge.

Diane had dabbled in Wicca as a teen, but the power that rose inside her now scared her. She was an adult and had put lucky charms and love potions behind her. So, why did she feel this strange calling to go out to the desert and…fly?

It just didn't make sense, but something had changed in recent days. Some power had awoken and was causing a reaction in her own soul. It was as if she was finally waking up after a long sleep, though why she felt that way, she had no idea.

Diane needed answers, but she didn't quite know how to go about getting them. She only knew that, somewhere out on the edge of town, she might find a clue. Now, the real question was, did she dare go after it?

# # #

ABOUT THE AUTHOR

Bianca D'Arc has run a laboratory, climbed the corporate ladder in the shark-infested streets of lower Manhattan, studied and taught martial arts, and earned the right to put a whole bunch of letters after her name, but she's always enjoyed writing more than any of her other pursuits. She grew up and still lives on Long Island, where she keeps busy with an extensive garden, several aquariums full of very demanding fish, and writing her favorite genres of paranormal, fantasy and sci-fi romance.

Bianca loves to hear from readers and can be reached through Twitter (@BiancaDArc), Facebook (BiancaDArcAuthor) or through the various links on her website.

WELCOME TO THE D'ARC SIDE…
WWW.BIANCADARC.COM

OTHER BOOKS
BY BIANCA D'ARC

Paranormal Romance

Brotherhood of Blood
One & Only
Rare Vintage
Phantom Desires
Sweeter Than Wine
Forever Valentine
Wolf Hills*
Wolf Quest

Tales of the Were
Lords of the Were
Inferno
Rocky
Slade

Tales of the Were ~ Redstone Clan
The Purrfect Stranger
Grif
Red
Magnus
Bobcat
Matt

Guardians of the Dark
Simon Says
Once Bitten
Smoke on the Water
Night Shade
Shadow Play

Gifts of the Ancients: Warrior's Heart

Gemini Project: Tag Team

Epic Fantasy Erotic Romance

Dragon Knights ~ Daughters of the Dragon
Maiden Flight*
Border Lair
The Ice Dragon**
Prince of Spies***

Dragon Knights ~ The Novellas
The Dragon Healer
Master at Arms
Wings of Change

Dragon Knights ~ Sons of Draconia
FireDrake
Dragon Storm
Keeper of the Flame
Hidden Dragons

Dragon Knights ~ The Sea Captain's Daughter
Sea Dragon
Dragon Fire
Dragon Mates

Science Fiction Romance

StarLords
Hidden Talent
Talent For Trouble
Shy Talent

Jit'Suku Chronicles ~ Arcana
King of Swords
King of Cups
King of Clubs
King of Stars
End of the Line
Diva

Jit'Suku Chronicles ~ Sons of Amber
Angel in the Badlands
Master of Her Heart

Jit'Suku Chronicles ~ In the Stars
The Cyborg Next Door

Futuristic Erotic Romance

* RT Book Reviews Awards Nominee
** EPPIE Award Winner
*** CAPA Award Winner

WWW.BIANCADARC.COM